KU-175-224

One Weird Day at
FREEKHAM HIGH
OUCH!

Steve Cole

OXFORD
UNIVERSITY PRESS

OXFORD
UNIVERSITY PRESS

Great Clarendon Street, Oxford OX2 6DP

Oxford University Press is a department of the University of Oxford.
It furthers the University's objective of excellence in research, scholarship,
and education by publishing worldwide in

Oxford New York

Auckland Cape Town Dar es Salaam Hong Kong Karachi
Kuala Lumpur Madrid Melbourne Mexico City Nairobi
New Delhi Shanghai Taipei Toronto

With offices in

Argentina Austria Brazil Chile Czech Republic France Greece
Guatemala Hungary Italy Japan Poland Portugal Singapore
South Korea Switzerland Thailand Turkey Ukraine Vietnam

Oxford is a registered trade mark of Oxford University Press
in the UK and in certain other countries

Text © Steve Cole 2005
Cover and inside illustrations © Lee White 2005

The moral rights of the author have been asserted

Database right Oxford University Press (maker)

First published 2005

All rights reserved. No part of this publication may be reproduced,
stored in a retrieval system, or transmitted, in any form or by any means,
without the prior permission in writing of Oxford University Press,
or as expressly permitted by law, or under terms agreed with the appropriate
reprographics rights organization. Enquiries concerning reproduction
outside the scope of the above should be sent to the Rights Department,
Oxford University Press, at the address above

You must not circulate this book in any other binding or cover
and you must impose this same condition on any acquirer

British Library Cataloguing in Publication Data

Data available

ISBN-13: 978-0-19-275426-4
ISBN-10: 0-19-275426-2

1 3 5 7 9 10 8 6 4 2

Typeset in Sabon by Palimpsest Book Production Limited,
Polmont, Stirlingshire

Printed in Great Britain by Cox & Wyman, Reading, Berkshire

Registration

As the boy fell off his chair for the third time in as many minutes, Sam Innocent laughed and led the class in a ragged round of applause.

'Nice one!' Fido Tennant gave a typically winning smile and paused the camcorder. 'That was a textbook stunt fall, Smithy!'

'Textbook!' Propping himself up on his elbows, Smithy stared around the classroom, seized by sudden inspiration. 'That's it! If I fell over into a big pile of textbooks it would be even funnier!'

As Smithy got busy ransacking a cupboard, Sam saw that his friend Sara Knot looked seriously unimpressed. In many ways the two of them were opposites; her eyes were wide and blue, his were oval and brown. Her nose was straight as a ski slope, his was short and snub. And while Sam could watch someone falling over

1

all day and not get bored, Sara was a good deal more sensible. She pursed her red lips, and her long blonde hair flicked around her shoulders as she shook her head wearily.

But they had things in common too. Freaky things. They were both born on February 29th of the same year. They had both started at Freekham High on the same day, just a few weeks ago. And since the two of them had got here, bizarre, peculiar events had started kicking off around the school.

It was almost as if the two of them were weird-magnets or something.

'OK,' said Smithy as he gleefully balanced a teetering pile of books beside his chair. His real name was Marcus Smythe, and he was a slightly podgy black guy with close-cropped hair who seemed to find a funny side to everything. He glanced around at his audience and rubbed his hands. 'Here I go again!'

'Doesn't it hurt, chucking yourself on the floor like that?' asked Sara.

'Nope.'

'How come?'

'I've got four older brothers,' Smithy explained.

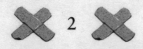

'Trust me, when your butt's been kicked as many times as mine, you don't feel a thing!'

'OK, tape's rolling,' Fido reported, blowing a wayward lock of brown hair from his eyes, his flash camcorder trained on Smithy. 'Ready when you are.'

Smithy started rocking casually on his chair, just as he had in the build up to each of his previous falls. Soon he 'accidentally' leant back a bit too far, and launched into his now-familiar routine. His eyes widened. His mouth turned down in dismay. His arms started windmilling as the chair toppled backwards and he fell sprawling into the tower of textbooks. Sam howled with laughter once more.

'Cool!' said Fido, snapping shut the hinged viewfinder screen. 'That cash is as good as ours. Just think, a hundred quid each!'

Sam wiped a tear from his eye and shrugged at Sara's disapproving frown. It seemed like a pretty good way to make money if you asked him. Fido fancied himself a bit of a film director, but before he could make his own movies, he needed some cash—and so had teamed up with Smithy, Freekham's resident stuntman. *Casey's*

Camcorder Catastrophes show on cable was offering £200 for funny video clips showing falls, slips, crashes, and general mayhem—provided no one taking part was hurt. So not only did you get cash for a smash, you got to be on TV too. A double-result and well worth a few bruises.

'That won't make it on Casey's show,' drawled Memphis Ball from her seat beside Sara. 'It looks too staged.' Memphis was tall and trim and bald as a billiard ball—her mum put it down to her going Buddhist but really she was just a rebel who'd shaved her head for the crack. Sam suspected she preferred watching life to taking part; but as a result, she had views on just about everyone in school, which was helpful to newbies like Sam and Sara.

'What do you mean, staged?' said Smithy indignantly as he scrambled up.

Memphis raised a plucked eyebrow; trained her stunning green eyes on him. 'Well, for a start, why would there be a massive heap of books in the middle of the classroom for you to fall into?'

Fido grimaced. 'She's got a point, Smithy.'

'I guess,' he grumbled, picking up the scattered books. 'Pity. That was a good one.'

'Tell you what,' said Fido, hitting some buttons on the back of the camcorder with easy precision. 'Let's review the footage, see what we've got so far . . .'

'Penter should be here any minute,' Sara warned them.

'Only if he's feeling better,' Sam pointed out. 'He's been off two days already.'

'I'm hoping he gets worse,' added Smithy.

Monday evening had been Teachers' Social Night, arranged by the Head. A bunch of them had gone out for a meal to help them 'bond' as a team. Sam had hoped that they might all bore each other to death, but the actual outcome had been much messier—twelve out of twenty had come down with food poisoning. So now, while the stricken teachers' toilets were awash with unmentionable horrors, the school was awash with things that were far, far worse—supply staff.

Fido gave a sudden snort of laughter, still staring at his camcorder. 'Look, Smithy! This is you this morning, doing the bike crash on the way to school!'

'Awesome!' Smithy yanked the camcorder off

Fido and Sam joined him, peering at the viewscreen.

There was Smithy, cycling along the street quite innocently, looking back over his shoulder at something. But as the camera moved to follow him, it showed he was heading for a gang of older boys loitering at the bottom of the school drive. One of them had more spots than a Dalmatian with measles.

'Isn't that Connor Flint, the Living Zit, and his bully boys?' Sam frowned. 'He's meant to be a bit evil. Taking a chance, weren't you?'

'Shut up and watch, you'll love this bit,' Smithy assured him.

Sam gasped as Smithy crashed into the middle of Connor's gang, scattering them like skittles before falling off his bike and somersaulting across the driveway.

'Ouch!' Sam winced. 'Impressive work, Smithy.'

'That's not the best bit, *look*!'

As Connor scrambled back to his feet, his trousers ripped wide open. The camera zoomed in to show a grotty pair of blue stripy boxers.

Sam and Smithy roared with laughter.

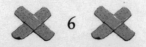

'Pretty cool, huh?' said Fido, craning his neck to see. 'Flint was *furious*! In front of all those people! Serves him right, he picks on so many kids . . .'

Sam kept watching the tape. 'Looks like he's going to pick on you, too!'

Connor was scowling as he turned to find Fido catching his pants on camera. He bunched his fists and started to stride over—and the picture wobbled and blurred as Fido beat a quick retreat.

'Did he catch up with you?' asked Sam.

'Nah,' Smithy said breezily. 'Anyway, he's all mouth, no ripped trousers. Come on, Fido, rewind it to yesterday lunchtime—the stunt in the caretaker's hut.'

Sam stared at them in amazement. 'You got in *there*?'

'Nowhere is safe from the Fido and Smithy faked disaster show!' said Fido as he worked the buttons.

'Especially when the old duffer keeps a key under the mat,' Smithy added.

'You guys are so lame,' sighed Sara. But she came over to see the stunt in any case.

Now the screen showed Smithy in front of a

pile of carefully stacked boxes. It looked as if he was searching for something on the floor. But suddenly he slipped and fell backwards into the boxes, which crashed down around him. And then a red-faced, bald-headed man in blue overalls entered the frame.

'You got caught!' said Sam. 'Red-handed! What happened?'

'Duh,' said Smithy. 'Keep watching and find out!'

The caretaker tried to grab hold of Smithy, but slipped in some spilled washing-up liquid and crashed to the floor.

'*Big* ouch!' chortled Smithy.

'Like, how totally clever,' said Sara drily.

Biggins's angry voice sounded thin and tinny through the camcorder's speakers, but there was no mistaking the rudeness of his words.

'You caught him swearing like that on tape!' Sam marvelled.

'That's why we didn't get into trouble,' said Fido sheepishly.

Smithy nodded with a crafty smile. 'I told him that if we got into trouble, we'd produce the tape as evidence.'

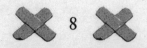

8

Sam couldn't believe his cheek. 'You never!'

He nodded cheerfully. 'Biggins decided he didn't want the Head knowing he'd said stuff like that to poor, impressionable pupils like us.'

'So that's two enemies you've made in as many days,' said Sara. 'You guys had better watch your backs.'

Smithy rolled his eyes. 'Lighten up, Knotty.'

'Don't call me Knotty!'

'You heard her,' said Sam. 'Do notty call her Knotty.' He and Smithy burst out into sniggers again.

'I'll just go back to the bike shed stunts at Breather yesterday,' said Fido, not joining in; Sam reckoned he was quite sweet on Sara. 'Those falls you did were pretty convincing, Smithy.'

'I nearly broke my legs, that's why!'

'Well, I reckon every one of these stunts is a money winner,' Sam observed. 'You should do some of them in disguise, Smithy, so you can send in more than one of them—get more money!'

Smithy turned to Sara. 'What d'you say, Knotty? Get your hair cut—I'll sweep it up and make a wig!'

 9

'Or maybe Ruth could donate some of her chest hair,' Sam suggested.

'I heard that, Innocent.' Ruth 'Ruthless' Cook glowered at him. She was the class thug, built like a rhino but with fewer brain cells. 'Want me to pull out your stupid spiky fringe one hair at a time?'

'Quick, Fido, get your tape running,' quipped Smithy. 'That's got to be worth two hundred pounds to *Casey's Camcorder Catastrophes*, right?'

Ruthless rose to her feet—but quickly sat back down as the door swung open and a towering woman in tweed barged inside, her heavy heels clicking on the classroom floor.

'No Penter again!' hissed Sam triumphantly. 'Yes!'

'But is Mrs Janus really much of an improvement?' Sara sighed, as the two of them returned to their places.

'All right, class, settle down,' Mrs Janus snapped in her deep booming voice. 'You're stuck with me again so let's all try to make the most of it.'

In Sam's experience, most supply teachers

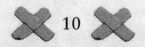

were weedy pushovers, more concerned with surviving the school day than actually trying to take lessons. But Mrs Janus was the exception. Perhaps because her preferred subject was Drama, she was very good at playing the tough nut. Her hair was all piled up on her head like a nest of snakes; her eyes glared from beneath heavy lids plastered in blue eyeshadow; her mouth was a slash of lipstick beneath her outsized nose, and her tweed skirt and jacket barely contained the various bits of her burly body. The rings on her left hand were so big they might have been knuckledusters— certainly you wouldn't want to find out for sure.

'Whatever you're looking at, Dorian, put it down,' she snapped.

Fido winced—probably at the use of his real name. He concealed his camcorder further under the table, but didn't pack it away. He and Smithy were too busy enjoying the show.

Sam had to admire their nerve. He, on the other hand, was keeping quiet today. He'd tried messing with Janus yesterday and she'd stomped on him. He'd received a detention in about six seconds flat, which was very nearly a personal best.

Janus went on to take the register—but when she called out Marcus Smythe, he could only manage a spluttering chuckle, his eyes glued to the footage. Clearly the bike shed stunt falls were good stuff.

'Right, I've had enough of this,' Janus boomed, striding towards them. 'Whatever the joke is, share it with the class.'

'They . . . uh . . . already offered it to us, miss,' said Sam, trying to buy Fido and Smithy time enough to lose the camcorder. 'We didn't want it.'

But Janus would not be distracted. 'What do you have there, Dorian?'

'Just my camcorder, miss,' said Fido, shutting it up and pushing it into his bag. 'Mr Steen asked me to bring it in today.'

'Oh, did he now?' She reached in and yanked the camcorder straight back out again. From the sound of the tinny voices, it was still playing. Janus stared at the screen for a few moments. Then her beady eyes widened, making her make-up crack.

'Right, you pair of little idiots,' she said,

suddenly flustered. 'I'm confiscating this.'

'But, miss, you can't!' Fido protested. He unfolded a piece of paper from his shirt pocket and handed it to her. 'Look, a note from Mr Steen to my mum, asking if I can bring it to Social Studies class. It's an emergency—the school one's broken down and I said I'd lend him mine. He needs to tape some workshops today for some visitors this afternoon.'

She crunched up the paper in her fist and dropped it. 'All right—I'll confiscate this tape!' She flipped the camcorder over, looking for the eject button. 'You're here to work, not watch yourselves fooling about!'

'You can't take that tape—it's the only one I've got!' said Fido quickly. 'Without that the camcorder's useless!'

She bore down on him. 'And when exactly *is* your lesson with Mr Steen?' she thundered.

'Next period, miss,' said Smithy, a bit shaken.

'I'll speak to Mr Steen myself at break,' she promised. 'The moment he's finished with it he'll hand it over to *me*.'

She started to pass him back the camcorder—but it slipped from her bejewelled hand. It

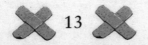

13

would have smashed on the polished tile floor if Smithy hadn't dived for it, just managing to curl the tips of his fingers around the straps.

He blew a long sigh of relief, and Fido grinned weakly. 'Butterfingers, miss.'

Janus's eyes had narrowed to blue slits. 'I'll be seeing you later, boys,' she hissed. Then she bustled back to her chair, a trail of stale perfume lingering in her wake.

At that moment, the hooter kicked off, warning the school of the start of lesson one. Its soundchip was broken and tricky to fix, and the weird honking noise usually raised a few smiles in class. But right now, no one dared move, watching Janus uncertainly.

'Go on, then, clear off, all of you!' she snapped.

Gratefully, the class complied—with Fido and Smithy leading the pack. Sam fell into step with Sara and Memphis.

'You were right, Sara,' Sam whispered. 'Come back, Penter, all is forgiven.'

Sara puffed out her cheeks. 'What's with her? That little show was just all-out freaky.'

'Yeah, it's weird,' said Memphis thoughtfully. 'I've had Janus before. She's not normally as uptight as that. Maybe she's had a row with her brother.'

Sam frowned. 'You know her *brother*? *Mr* Janus?'

'Janus is a *Mrs*, dork-brain. Didn't you see the bling on her finger?'

'It's an engagement ring, isn't it?' said Sara.

Memphis nodded. 'And the one next to it is her wedding band.'

'*She* should be banned if you ask me,' Sam grumbled.

'Her maiden name is Bruce,' Memphis went on. 'She used to be an actor, she reckons, Belinda Bruce—but she packed it in when she got married.'

Sam wasn't impressed. 'In other words, she was rubbish and never got anywhere.'

'You can judge for yourself—we've got her for Drama after lunch. Anyway, her brother is *Mr* Bruce, the supply PE teacher.'

'Is he a failed actor too?'

'He's filling in for Mrs Hurst while she's sick. Guess he'll be taking us for Games after breather.'

'Can't wait,' Sara sighed.

'What are the odds of a brother and sister both being supply teachers and both at the same

school?' Sam marvelled. 'Reckon they come from a whole family of educational substitutes?'

'Why not? This *is* Freekham High,' Sara reminded him. 'Where weird stuff goes to happen.'

'Since you two turned up, anyway,' said Memphis, her green eyes sparkling.

Periods One and Two
Social Studies

Fido and Smithy were first in line outside Softy Steen's room. Sara, Sam, and Memphis went over to join them.

'So is that really the only tape you have?' Sam asked.

'Looks like it.' Fido frowned. 'Funny, I could have sworn I'd packed another one. But there's no sign of it anywhere.'

'Dodgy,' said Smithy. 'I thought you were tricking old Janus. But now you'll really have to give old Softy our stunt tape!'

'Don't worry, I'll zero the tape at the end of the fall footage,' said Fido. 'It'll automatically stop there when Steen rewinds. That way, he won't see what we've been up to.'

'You hope,' said Sara pointedly. 'Especially that stuff with the caretaker.'

Just then, the classroom door opened and Softy

 17

Steen peered out. He was a skinny, serious look-ing young man with a wispy blond beard. Being a lactose-intolerant vegan, he'd apparently escaped the food poisoning by eating dry toast all evening. With his threadbare blazer, mismatched shirt and tie, and yellow flares, you'd think he'd been left to dress himself blindfolded in an Oxfam shop. But it seemed this was just Steen's teacherly way of telling the world he was an *individual*. Or as Sam put it more realistically: a *prat*.

'You've brought the camcorder!' Steen beamed at Fido. 'Wicked, guy, you've saved my life.'

Sara winced. Steen was one of those teachers who tried desperately to be your friend. He always spoke as if he was 'down with the kids'. He *so* wasn't. But while he was a bit cringeworthy, he was definitely one of the better teachers around, and mostly harmless.

As she went inside, she saw the tables and chairs had been rearranged into a half-circle, leaving a larger area at the front. A tripod stood by his desk—no guesses where Fido's camcorder would end up.

'What do you need it for, sir?' wondered Fido. 'What's this meeting?'

18

'I have some school psychoanalysts hanging with me this afternoon. You know . . .' He mimed quotation marks with his fingers as he said, 'Therapists. Shrinks. They can't make it to today's lesson, so I'm going to video your performances.'

Sam took a seat and looked at Steen warily. 'Performances for, like, proper analysts to watch?'

'Sure! We're doing some role-play this morning.' Steen smiled. 'I've come up with the idea of a new kind of self-help club. One that's run *by* kids, *for* kids. It's called SHAPE—Self-Help Against Parental Embarrassment. Pretty rad, huh?'

'Rad. Right.' Sara smiled at Memphis beside her. 'So it's like Alcoholics Anonymous or something, only for kids who are shown up by their parents.'

'Spot on, Sara,' Steen agreed. 'See, I know how embarrassed you guys get by your parents. Grown-ups don't mean to be uncool and shameful, but they are—and they find it hard to take when you try to tell them. But SHAPE will offer young adults like you the chance to sound off in a consequence-free environment.'

Sam winced. 'That sounds more embarrassing than anything my parents could do.'

 19

'Don't deny till you try, Sam!' Steen wagged a limp finger. 'Your fellow pupils can sympathize, share their own experiences, and even suggest ways of improving things. Those are the three golden rules of SHAPE: air—share—care.'

'And puke over there,' added Sam, miming a finger down his throat.

'I think it sounds like a good idea,' countered Ashley Lamb, Sam's deskmate. He'd been branded *loser* most of his school life, but now he'd finally stopped sucking his thumb he'd been given an upgrade to *OK but a bit lame*. 'If grown-ups blame their problems on their kids, they get therapy. But if kids blame their problems on their parents they get sent to their room!'

Suddenly Sara felt Memphis's elbow in her ribs. 'But who's sent *her* to *our* room?'

Sara followed her gaze and, through the glass in the classroom door, saw someone hovering outside. It was Mrs Janus, peering in to see what was happening. Her caked blue eyes soon fixed on the camcorder beside Softy Steen, and hardened.

'She must be checking up on Fido's story,' Sara realized. 'God, what is her problem?'

 20

'Well, she *is* a teacher,' Sam quietly pointed out as the scowling figure turned from the door and vanished. 'Where'd you want to start?'

Fido was still gassing to Steen, utterly oblivious. 'Things seem to be kicking off a bit fast, sir,' he observed. 'Like, you only asked to borrow the camcorder yesterday.'

'That's because I only knew about the meeting yesterday,' he explained. 'These analyst guys, they're, like, heavy regional bigwigs. Busy people. But yesterday, a gap opened up in their diary so they've slotted me in.' He seemed to be sweating a little, and ran a hand nervously through his beard. 'It's not ideal—I mean, the school video camera's busted, I've got training all the rest of the morning and I haven't really prepared, but . . . well, I'm running out of time if I want to try and get SHAPE introduced into other schools around the county for the autumn term.'

Sara frowned at Memphis. 'What is this, Teacher Confessions? Are we his analysts now?'

She smiled wickedly. 'No, we're just his dear young adult buddies.'

Steen flashed an awkward smile around the class. 'Well, enough chat. I think it's time we all got into

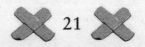

21

SHAPE! Vicki, let's have you out in front please.'

As Vicki Starling stepped forwards, all blue eyes, dimpled cheeks, and platinum blonde bunches, it was Sara's turn to mime a finger down her throat. Vicki was Miss Perfect; she was *always* out in front.

'Is there anything your parents do that embarrasses you?' Steen asked.

'My dad . . .' She shuddered. 'He goes . . . clubbing.'

'What, clubbing fur seals you mean?' said Sam, perking up.

Vicki put her hands on her hips. '*Night*clubbing, you doofus. Twice a week!'

'Let's have Smithy down here, too,' said Steen. Smithy frowned. 'Me?'

'Uh-huh. I want you to pretend you're Vicki's dad.'

He joined her in the performing space. 'So, can I boss her around?'

'Good luck!' was Vicki's caustic response.

'OK, now, Vicki, this is a consequence-free environment.' He leaned over to the camcorder and switched it on. 'So just say to Smithy the things you'd love to tell your dad.'

Vicky wasted no time whatsoever.

'Dad, you have to stop being so *desperate*,' she yelled at Smithy. 'Dancing is for young people. You are over forty-five: you are not allowed to be trendy by law, so why even try?'

'Hey, girl, don't mock—I rock! Check out these moves!' Smithy started dancing like a mad uncle at a wedding disco. But Sara saw a sneaky glance pass between him, Fido, and the camera, and a second later he pretended to slip. He banged his head on the chalkboard and his bum on the floor, then flailed about on his back to a few weak titters.

'He just can't stop himself, can he,' remarked Memphis.

'Sir, Smithy's not taking it seriously!' Vicki complained.

'Smithy, take it seriously.'

'Yes, sir,' he said, getting back up. 'Sorry, daughter.'

Vicki tried again: 'Why can't you just stay in with Mum and wear a suit and be boring like other dads?'

'I've asked your mum to come clubbing with me and the lads,' said Smithy, pretending to

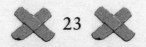

wipe an eye. 'She always says no.'

'That's because she has *dignity*!' Vicki shouted. 'And a bad hip. Anyway, they're not "lads" you go out with—they're accountants!'

'Vicki,' Steen broke in, 'it's great that you're letting out your anger, but remember you want a positive result from this confrontation. So what do we need here?'

Tranquillizers, thought Sara.

Vicky sucked a finger as she considered. 'I guess I need to draw up a checklist of achievable demands and, if necessary, negotiate a compromise.'

'Sweet!' Steen beamed, giving her a thumbs up.

'She is *such* a crawler,' muttered Memphis.

'Hey, baby, I know what'll make all this better—a nice, big hug!' Smithy advanced on Vicki with his arms outstretched. 'Come to papa!'

With a cry of revulsion, Vicki shoved him away. He fell to the floor again and launched into a spectacular backwards roll.

Steen scowled. 'Smithy, just chill out, OK? I've got to show this tape to the analysts!'

Sara heard Fido snigger softly. 'Yeah, but *we've* got to show it to Casey's cable show!'

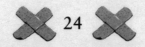

'OK, tape's rolling again,' said Steen. 'Let's pick up where we left off. Checklist of demands.'

Vicki wagged her finger at Smithy, and slowly advanced. 'Point one: do *not* go down Glitzy's and dance with your shirt undone *ever* again. Point two: do *not* try to talk to my friends about our music like you know *anything* about it.' Her voice was rising as if someone had sat on the volume control of her remote. 'And when you're giving us a lift somewhere, don't *ever* quote lines from our fave shows like you get what we're into or something—'cause you *don't*!'

'OK, fine, whatever!' Smithy stormed over to a window and fumbled with the catch. 'You want to speak up a little? Only, you know, I think someone in Norway missed what you said. How about we open this and you can yell it out all over again!'

Steen rolled his eyes as Smithy struggled with the stiff catch to open the window. 'Er, *Daddy*, it'd be cool if you could just try to reason—'

'Reason? With *that*?' He stared into the camera and shook his head in horror. 'I've raised a monster! After all I've done for her, she . . .

she . . .' He clutched his chest and slowly sank to the floor as if he was having some kind of attack, hamming it up for all he was worth.

'All right, Smithy, you've gone too far, mate,' snapped Steen, blushing furiously and staring at the floor. 'Just . . . just go and stand outside please, yeah?'

Smithy sat up and stared at him in surprise. 'You serious?'

'Yes, I am, actually,' said Steen, switching off the camcorder. 'I don't want to be negative but you're bringing us all down, mate. So if you don't mind, just go outside, please, and stay there for the rest of the lesson. If that's all right with you, I mean. Er . . . OK?'

Smithy seemed to consider for a few moments. Then he shrugged and did as he was told, shutting the door behind him.

'Poor old Smithy,' whispered Sara. 'How embarrassing—bawled out by Softy Steen!'

Memphis smiled. 'He'll probably have to join SHAPE to help him get over it.'

'OK, well . . .' Steen smoothed his hands through his hair, set the camcorder recording and tried to smile as if nothing had happened. 'Now

Dad's cut and run, does anyone have any advice for Vicki?'

'I do,' said Therese Briggs, raising her hand. She was part of Vicki's 'chic clique' and probably her most adoring fan. 'Vicki should become, like, a movie star—she'd be a natural. Then she could live in a mansion in Hollywood and she wouldn't care about her dad.'

'Aww, thanks, T'reez!' grinned Vicki.

Steen sighed heavily. 'That's a sweet thought, Therese, but I was thinking of something more practical.'

'She could chin the old idiot,' suggested Ruth Cook. 'Or trip him up at the top of the stairs. Reckon that would stop him dancing.'

'Doubt it,' said 'Doubting' Thomas Doughty, who didn't believe in anything much. 'He'd keep going. But he'd have, like, a really embarrassing limp or something that would make things even worse.'

Steen switched off the camcorder with a despairing look. 'OK, guys, let's take five while I explain the point of all this again . . .'

The lesson wore on. Sara was asked to raise some issues with her mother, played today by

mousy Michelle Harris. Sara complained that her mum moved around too much with her job—Freekham was the second school she'd been to this year. But within a few moments Michelle was blushing crimson and welling up with tears, saying it wasn't her fault, so Steen had to switch off the camcorder again.

Sam had it worse. He was picked to play Ruth's dad, who apparently embarrassed her by not putting on an acceptably rough accent when buying drinks in pubs. Unfortunately for both Sam and Mr Steen, Ruth's idea of negotiation and compromise was to offer him a choice between a punch in the face or the stomach. Yet again, the tape was switched off and the role-play concluded in the nick of time. And poor old Smithy had to watch the whole thing through the glass in the door, shut out and all-but-forgotten.

Still, as period two drew to a close, Steen seemed cautiously happy. 'I think I've got enough to show my visitors this afternoon—thanks, guys. And a big up to you, Fido, for letting me hang on to the camcorder, yeah? I'll edit out all the mistakes when I dub it down to videotape at lunchtime, after my course. Shouldn't take too long.'

'I'll rewind it to the right place for you, sir,' said Fido with a wink at Sam. 'Wouldn't want to bore you with the junk on the start of this tape—'

But just then, there was a massive crashing sound from outside the classroom. Steen jumped about a metre in the air.

'What was that?' gasped Sara, as the class burst out in wondering whispers and giggles.

'Oh my gosh, I totally forgot about Smithy!' Steen stared at the door, looking stricken with guilt. 'Poor guy's been outside all this time . . .'

'Better check he's all right, sir,' said Sam, taking the initiative as usual and heading for the classroom door.

Then the hooter sounded for the end of period two, and the class exploded into action, grabbing bags, scraping chairs, and shoving past desks.

Sara was first out after Sam. First she saw white crockery smashed all over the floor. Then she saw the tea trolley lying on its side, and a steaming brown puddle slowly filling the corridor.

 29

And then she saw Sam crouched down beside Smithy—sprawled face down on the tea-spattered floor.

BREAKTIME

'It's all right,' Sam reported to the class. 'He's just dazed, I think.'

'Dazed? I was squashed flat!' groaned Smithy, wincing as he rolled over onto some shattered saucers. 'This was a hit and run! Did anyone get the number plate of that truck?'

'Why?' said Therese. 'Do you collect them or something?'

'Sorry, Smithy,' said Sara. 'It was just an un-licensed tea trolley.'

Smithy let Sam help him up, rubbing the small of his back. 'If only you'd got it on tape, Fido!'

'Yeah,' Fido agreed. 'Then we'd know who shoved that thing into you.'

'No, I mean *then* we'd have a *real* accident to send in to Casey!' he wailed. 'We'd get the cash easy!'

Sara frowned. 'So you didn't see anyone?'

31

He shook his head. 'All I saw was stars.'

'Was anyone else out here?'

'Killer Collier passed through with some kids from the year below.' He gestured along the corridor. 'But that was a while ago, and they all went into a classroom down there.'

Softy Steen emerged from the classroom to take charge with all the enthusiasm of a hermit crab. 'Er . . . someone get Smithy a chair,' he suggested. 'He's had a bit of a shock.'

Smithy scowled. 'A bit of a *knock*, you mean.'

Another class was spilling out into the corridor now, younger kids gassing on about the weather experiments they'd just been doing outside. Since any excitement seemed to be over, Sam's class-mates began to drift away with them.

Then Sam heard a door slam open behind him. 'Nobody move! Everyone stay exactly where you are!'

The corridor fell silent. Sam froze at the furious voice. He almost raised his hands, half-expecting some gun-wielding robber come to take them all hostage.

In actual fact it was Biggins the caretaker, bursting out from the boys' toilets. He was not

a handsome man at the best of times, since his usual expression was that of an OAP trying to swallow prunes in vinegar. But he looked positively petrifying in a pop-eyed rage, his wrinkled old neck wobbling like a turkey's, his red cheeks and pink pate glowing like neon.

'What's going on here?' he demanded. 'Who's vandalized my tea trolley?'

The stunned crowd soon recovered their wits and most of them pressed on, trying not to laugh as they fled from the crime scene. Sara and Memphis hung back with a few others.

'Er . . .' Steen swallowed hard, a little taken aback. 'This is *your* trolley, Mr Biggins?'

'Of course it's mine!' he raged. 'I was on my way to the staffroom—bringing fresh tea for you lot, since the normal feller's off sick. Only left the trolley for a couple of minutes while I went and spent a penny. Now I come back and find . . .' Biggins peered at Smithy and Fido. 'Well, well. Might have known you two would be up to no good.'

'It's nothing to do with me!' Fido protested. 'I was in the classroom!'

Ruthless Cook stepped forwards, smiling

 33

nastily. 'Smithy wasn't though. He was standing out here—got thrown out for mucking about.'

Steen looked kind of flustered. 'Er . . . let's all take a chill pill, OK? I really don't think that Smithy—'

'Well, lad?' glowered Biggins, taking a more direct approach with the suspect. 'Are you *sure* you know nothing more about this?'

'No, I don't!' As Ruth strutted off smugly, Smithy looked between Steen and the caretaker crossly. 'It's not my fault I didn't see who shoved that thing into me! I'm the victim here, not the criminal!'

'Look, we all know that blame is lame, right, Mr Biggins?'

'Wrong, Mr Steen,' snapped Biggins. 'And whoever made this mess, it needs to be tidied up!' He pointed at Fido and Smithy. 'Reckon these two can do it. They're nearest.'

'But that's not fair!' Fido complained. 'Smithy's hurt himself!'

Steen too opened his mouth as if he was going to object, but Biggins fixed him with a murderous glare and his nerve broke. 'Mr B has a point, guys. Er . . . Sam, perhaps you'd give them a hand, eh?'

34

Sam stared incredulously. 'Why me?'

'Many hands make light work.'

'But too many cooks spoil the broth.'

Sara smiled. 'Ah, but this is *tea*!'

'And it's *already* spoiled,' said Biggins. 'So get cleaning!' He sank his hands deep in his pockets and a satisfied smile spread over his face. 'You'll find a mop and some bin liners in the storeroom down the corridor. Now, I'll have to go and find *another* trolley. And I shan't let *this* one out of my sight!' With that, he turned and bustled away, muttering under his breath.

'Thanks, guys,' said Steen, looking at them apologetically. 'Sorry to lay this rap on you, but I don't want people accusing me of going soft just 'cause you lent me your camcorder, Fido.' He locked the door to his classroom and set off for the staffroom. 'Laters, yeah?'

'Yeah, laters, "bro",' sighed Smithy. 'Thanks for nothing!'

'Old Biggins was taking a chance, wasn't he?' Sara observed. 'You've still got him going off into one on tape, you could drop him right in it.'

'Not without dropping ourselves in it too,' said Fido ruefully.

 35

Smithy nodded. 'Sneaking into his hut, mucking about . . . Head would go mental.'

'And Biggins knows that, the old curmudgeon,' said Fido. 'Like he knows the only way to get back at us is *indirectly*.'

Sam looked at him. 'You think it was *Biggins* who pushed that trolley into Smithy?'

Fido shrugged. 'Well, it *was* his trolley. And he did steer it all the way here before conveniently nipping into the bogs.'

'Maybe it was an accident,' said Sara.

'You saw him on the tape,' Smithy retorted, stooping to pick up some broken cups. 'He's got a real temper on him.'

'Hang on.' Sara frowned. 'You've got something sticking out of your back pocket. A piece of paper or something.'

Smithy felt for the paper and smiled craftily. 'You checking out my booty, Knotty?'

She folded her arms. 'Sure. Like an exterminator might check out a bug.'

'Looks like someone's slipped you a note, Smithy,' Sam observed. 'What's it say?'

'Dunno. I've never seen it before . . .' He scanned the paper and his face grew serious.

He passed the note to Sam, and the others crowded round to see.

> Leave the tape under the crash mats at the start of lunchtime—or there'll be more hilarious accidents

'*Biggins* must have stuck it in my pocket,' breathed Smithy, 'after he shoved the trolley at me!'

'Looks like our caretaker wants to take care of *you*!' said Fido uneasily.

'Why only me?' Smithy complained. 'You were there too!'

'But I wasn't standing out here, was I,' said Fido, fiddling absent-mindedly with the back of his trousers. 'Anyway, be fair, it was *you* who gave him all that lip yesterday.'

'Yeah, and saved your butt from getting a roasting!'

'Look, you don't know for sure that the note even came from Biggins,' said Sam.

'It could have been anyone,' added Sara. 'Connor Flint for instance.'

'He'd have been in lessons,' Memphis pointed

out. 'And what are the chances of him happening upon that trolley at the exact moment Biggins popped to the toilets . . . ?'

'I just can't believe Biggins would deliberately hurt one of us,' said Sara firmly.

'Anyway, what are you going to do,' said Sam. 'Put the tape under the crash mats like it says?'

'How can we?' said Fido glumly. 'Steen's got the tape, remember—and he's not going to start editing his footage till lunchtime!'

'Whatever, we can't let him get away with this,' Smithy declared. 'We'll just have to stick close together and watch out for him. He won't dare try anything in public.'

'In the meantime, we'd better get this lot cleared up,' sighed Fido. 'If we're late for Geography, Collier will throw more than tea trolleys at us.'

Sam looked hopefully at Sara and Memphis. 'We'd finish faster if you gave us a hand.'

The girls started clapping. 'A *big* hand for the Freekham clean-up victims,' said Sara. '*Adios!*'

Sam sighed as the two of them walked off. 'I'll fetch the mop.'

'I'll come with you,' said Fido.

'Slackers!' Smithy called after them.

Sam opened the storeroom door—and a bundle of boxes spilled out at his feet. It looked as if the place had been turned upside down.

'What a mess!' he complained. 'Did you and Smithy pull one of your stunts in here?'

'Course not! It's Biggins's job to keep the store-rooms tidy, isn't it?' said Fido. 'I reckon he's lost the plot!'

'Either that or . . .' Sam gulped, 'he's messed it up deliberately—something else he can blame on us!'

'Oh, no,' groaned Fido. 'We'll have to tidy *this* up too, so he can't drop us in it!'

'What's this "we"?' Sam enquired. 'None of this vendetta stuff has got anything to do with me!'

'Thought you were a mate,' Fido retorted.

Sam sighed and nodded. 'OK. But if this *is* down to Biggins . . . how long till he gets it out of his system?'

Fido nodded gloomily. 'End of term is still three weeks away.'

'But Geography is a lot closer,' sighed Sam, pulling the mop and bucket from beneath a pile

of paper towels. 'And it's no good crying over spilled tea. Let's get on with it.'

'I just can't believe Biggins would attack a pupil,' Sara insisted as they walked down the corridor of the humanities block.

Memphis yawned. 'Yeah, so you said. Five times already.'

'Well, can you?'

'I've never heard of him picking on anyone else,' Memphis admitted. 'Normally keeps himself to himself. But then again, Smithy *is* incredibly annoying.'

'Mmm,' said Sara. 'I don't know why Fido hangs with him.'

Memphis pouted. 'What, when he could be hanging with *you* instead?'

'Get lost!' Sara protested, feeling her cheeks redden. 'Anyway, we were talking about Biggins.'

'Well, if you're so desperate to prove his innocence—'

'It's not that. It's just that if Smithy and Fido start watching out for Biggins and it's *not* him, it means that whoever *did* do it is still about—

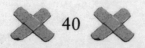

and no one's watching them at all.' Sara frowned. 'And yeah, Smithy is *really* irritating, but I still don't want to see him get hurt.'

'No, he'll manage that all by himself with those dumb stunt falls of his!' said Memphis. 'Hey, I know what might shed some light on this. We find something with Biggins's handwriting on, and compare it to the note left in Smithy's pocket.'

'Whoever wrote the note probably *disguised* their writing.'

'Yeah, but it's very hard to *completely* disguise your handwriting,' Memphis argued. 'Especially since they didn't use capitals.'

'Shh!' said Sara. They'd turned a corner in the corridor, and standing by the doors outside were Softy Steen and Mrs Janus.

'I'm really sorry, Belinda,' Steen was saying guiltily. Clearly he saved his 'cool' chat for his pupils—in private he was just as straight-laced as his fellow teachers. 'I can't let you have the tape or the camcorder just yet. They're locked in my classroom, and I won't be finished with them till after lunch.'

'But you've finished your filming, haven't you?'

'Yes, but now I have to edit my footage for

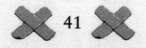

a very important meeting this afternoon.'

Janus did not look happy at the news. 'Well, I think it's outrageous that pupils should be allowed to wander the school with a camcorder, taping whatever they like! Beastly devices, they're an invasion of privacy!'

'I *did* ask Fido to bring the camcorder in—'

'Yes, and very irresponsible of you it was too,' said Janus. 'What if someone steals it? You asked him to bring it in—the school will be liable! Do you know how much one of those things costs?'

Steen raised himself up to his full height, which still only brought his eyes up to Janus's chin. 'Mrs Janus, I see where you're coming from, yeah? But the camcorder is locked away, so no one can get to it. And I won't give it back to Fido until after school—is that OK?'

'I'm not at all pleased with your casual approach to this problem,' fumed Janus. 'I shall collect the camcorder from you after lunch, and *I'll* give it back to Dorian Tennant myself—along with a very stern lecture!'

'If that's the way you have to play,' sighed Steen meekly. 'I need to get going. Bye for now.'

With that, he excused himself and forced his

way through the double doors to freedom. Janus stayed fuming for a few moments, then she headed off after him.

'She's really gone mental over this camcorder thing,' Memphis mused. 'Normally she's all right, just a bit of a pain. Nothing as full-on as this.'

'Camcorders must be a pet hate, I guess,' said Sara. 'You know, like Kale loathes Walkmans, and Penter despises pupils.' Suddenly she gasped. 'Hey, you don't think *Janus* pushed the trolley into . . . ?'

As the hooter sounded for the end of break, Memphis looked at her doubtfully. '*I* think it's lucky we've got Geography next.'

'Why?'

''Cause your imagination's obviously running away with you,' she grinned, 'and at least if you know the local geography you might find out where it's taking you!'

Periods Three and Four
Geography

Wiping his freshly-cleaned hands on his shirt, Sam hurried into Collier's classroom just behind Fido and Smithy. It had been hard work, but they'd done a pretty good job of cleaning up the mess, both out in the corridor and inside the storeroom. No way could Biggins blame them for that bit of vandalism now.

It rankled with Sam, though, having to slave away through his break. Fair enough, a mate was a mate, but Fido and Smithy had got themselves into these messes—and they could clean up after themselves next time.

Even so, Sam had to admit he loved a mystery, and the identity of the threatening note-writer was a juicy one. It was nice to be able to put his brainpower to good use for a change, instead of the usual boring class work.

'Hurry up and sit down, lads,' snapped Killer

44

Collier, hunched behind his cluttered desk in his habitual navy blue pinstripes. Despite being short, shrivelled, and about a million years old he had a fearful presence about him, and a voice that could out-shout thunder. 'Today, we're continuing our work on weather systems by studying different kinds of wind.'

'Mine stinks,' sniggered Smithy.

'We know,' said Vicki Starling coldly from the desk behind him.

'This will build on the work we've been doing on the Beaufort Scale,' Collier went on.

The class looked confused and Sam wondered why. 'We did the Beaufort Scale last year!' Fido explained. 'Collier must be having one of his flashbacks.'

'His what?'

'He has them sometimes,' said Smithy. 'He's mental. Should have retired ages ago!'

'Shouldn't we say something?' Sam wondered.

'Why should we?' Smithy grinned. 'We can copy out last year's homework and he'll be none the wiser!'

'You'll need your rough books and a pen,' said Collier, 'as we'll be going outside to the

weather station in order to record—'

'*Yowwwwwl!*' shrieked Fido, snatching his hand from his bag and doing a bizarre jig around Sam's desk. The class broke out into startled laughter—until Collier creaked into a standing position in a faint cloud of chalk dust.

'Mr Tennant,' he roared. 'What is the meaning of this outburst?'

Fido stared at him, cheeks red and hot and with tears in his eyes. 'Nothing, sir. Just—just really thrilled to be going out to the weather station.' He held up a jubilant fist. 'Whoop!'

Collier scowled, his thick white moustache bristling beneath his nose like a sociopathic caterpillar. 'Any more nonsense from you, Mr Tennant, and I'll put you in detention from now until term's end, do I make myself clear?'

'Crystal clear, sir,' gasped Fido, sitting down beside Sam. Sam saw his fingers—they were bright red and starting to swell.

'What happened?' he whispered, as Collier waffled on about what they'd be doing.

'*This* thing happened!'

Fido produced something small and wooden from his bag. It was a mousetrap, one of the

old-fashioned spring-loaded kind. Sam winced—Fido's fingers must have set it off and got properly whacked by the wire. He picked it up and turned it over: PROPERTY OF FREEKHAM HIGH was stamped on the back in aged ink, but nothing else.

'Hey, if this mousetrap belongs to the school, it must have been kept somewhere,' said Sam quietly. 'Somewhere like that storeroom we just tidied! Whoever made the mess in there could have fetched this at the same time!'

Fido nodded and passed over a piece of paper with his good hand. 'This came with it, taped to the side.'

No excuses. Tape under the crash mats, start of lunchtime.

'Smithy will be pleased,' said Sam uneasily. 'He's not the only one being picked on, after all.'

'All right, class, follow me,' said Collier. 'Single-file crocodile, and no talking!'

As the class milled about unenthusiastically to form a line, Smithy, Sara, and Memphis made a beeline over to see what the fuss was about.

 47

Fido discreetly showed them the mousetrap.

'Ouch!' said Sara in sympathy. 'Why didn't you tell Collier what really happened?'

Fido gave her a look. 'What, and risk having to explain this note away?'

'Where's the one you got, Smithy?' Smithy passed it to Sara and she compared them closely. 'Handwriting matches,' she noted, passing them to Memphis. 'Whoever wrote these, they're keen to get hold of that tape, aren't they?'

Smithy nodded gravely. 'And the last thing we need is Collier finding out about it. If he sees what we've got up to on there . . .'

Fido winced. 'He might not remember that caning's been banned!'

'Come on, get a move on,' snarled Collier from the corridor. 'Or I'll get out my cane!'

Memphis quickly shoved the notes in her bag as they all shuffled towards the door, joining the tail end of the class.

'That mousetrap wasn't there when I packed away in Steen's lesson,' muttered Fido. 'Someone played this little trick at break.'

'Where did you leave your bag?' asked Sara.

'With Sam's and Smithy's, outside Steen's

classroom. We took the trolley back to the staffroom and came back to collect them.'

Memphis nodded. 'So that's when it happened.'

'Biggins would have known where the mousetrap was,' said Smithy gravely.

'But the storeroom door was unlocked,' Sam countered. 'Anyone could have gone in there.'

'Why would they want to?'

Sara clicked her fingers. 'Maybe whoever shoved the trolley into you hid in there afterwards!'

Sam nodded slowly. 'We didn't see any sign of anyone, did we? They could have slipped away in the crowds when everyone left their lessons.'

'With a mousetrap in their pocket?' Fido nodded slowly. 'Maybe they turned that storeroom upside down looking for something like that to get me with!'

'I still reckon it's Biggins,' said Smithy stubbornly.

'Well, it's kind of good news in a way.' Memphis looked at Sara and tapped her bag. 'Means we've got two pieces of handwriting to check against.'

Seeing the boys' blank faces, Memphis and Sara explained their plan to either identify or

 49

eliminate Biggins as note-writing prime suspect.

'But where are you going to find anything with his handwriting on?' asked Smithy.

'There must be *something* in his hut,' said Sara.

Sam smiled. 'If he keeps his key beneath the mat, maybe we can sneak in and take a look at Breather.'

Just then, the conversation had to stop. Collier was waiting for the last stragglers, one gnarled hand clutching an old carpetbag, and a fierce glint still showing in his rheumy old eyes.

Sara had yet to visit Freekham's weather station, just off one of the main walkways. It was a grand name for what was actually a little bricked-in paddock behind the school's electricity supply. It held a thermometer for showing temperature, a barometer for measuring air pressure, and a metal trough stabbed with dipsticks for recording rainfall, built into the top of a low, slatted cupboard. In a gust of wind that set Sara's blonde locks whipping out around her, one of the doors blew open to reveal a pile of odds and ends inside. Collier crossly slammed it back shut.

Over the wall, she noticed Mrs Janus hurrying off somewhere, probably late for her lesson. A group of kids passed her in the opposite direction, coming Sara's way. They were led by Mr Ferret who took Agricultural Studies, and were presumably heading for the school farm.

'Now then,' said Collier, opening his carpetbag. 'I want you to get into groups of four and devise different ways for measuring the wind using the tools in here.'

Sara peered into the ragbag assortment. Vicki Starling was first to delve in, grabbing a small anemometer to share with her chic clique. Memphis calmly took a protractor, a piece of string, and a ping-pong ball with the air of someone who knew what they were doing, and both Michelle Harris and little Ginger Mutton gravitated towards her.

'We did this last year,' Ginger explained quietly, her lank copper hair catching on her chunky glasses in a fresh gust. 'It's cool. You tape the ping-pong ball to the string—'

'Mmm, sounds like fun,' said Sara with a polite smile. While Collier had gone to lecture Vicki's group on their piece of precision equipment, she

saw that all Sam, Smithy, Fido, and Ashley had been left with was an old stripy sock—a *wind*-sock, she supposed.

Fido dangled it doubtfully from thumb and forefinger. 'How can a sock be called a tool?'

'Oh, I dunno,' said Smithy. 'Some of my old socks could knock you unconscious. Useful tool for bank robbers.' His group duly chuckled.

'Good one,' came a voice from over the top of the weather station wall. It was a small kid with a buzz cut, who'd broken away from Ferret's group to see them. He wore a pair of thick round glasses and a smirk.

'Er . . . do we know you?' Sam enquired.

'The name's Linus—and I guess you'd prefer to be dangling a pair of *pants*, there, huh, Fido?' he said, grinning knowingly. 'Or do I mean a pair of stripy boxers!'

Now Fido smiled back. 'I get it! You saw our stunt this morning!'

'Uh-huh,' said Linus. 'And I want to thank you for what you did to Connor Flint. It was perfect!'

'The ripped trousers bit was just an accident,' said Smithy. 'But I guess it did turn out pretty perfect, didn't it?'

 52

'Did the tape come out OK?' Linus asked eagerly. 'Have you shown it to, like, loads of people?'

'A few,' Fido admitted, pulling distractedly at the seat of his trousers.

'I've seen it,' said Sam. 'It's really cool.'

'Wow,' said Linus. 'I bet Connor would do *anything* to get that tape back!'

'Linus Smellick, get back here!' called Mr Ferret, a big bear of a man with a temper to match. 'You've already had your lesson with Mr Collier—now pay attention to mine!'

'*We* had to stand around out here with him too,' said Linus, starting back. 'Boring or what? Well, see you around.' He tossed a cheeky smile back over his shoulder. 'Maybe you'll show me the tape at lunchtime, huh?'

Fido and Smithy looked grimly at each other. 'Maybe,' they chorused.

'How about that,' Sara marvelled as Linus dashed back to rejoin his group. 'You've got your first fan!'

'Yeah, never mind *Casey's Camcorder Catastrophes*,' Sam smiled, 'you could be heading for your own show!'

 53

'Or another "hilarious accident",' sighed Fido. 'If we don't get that tape off Steen and leave it under the crash mats.'

'Look out,' Sam whispered. 'Collier's looking this way.'

Sara and Memphis nudged back towards Ginger and Michelle, who were sorting out the ping-pong protractor. Memphis grabbed hold of it, pretending to study it closely.

'From what that kid was saying, sounds like Collier's just taken a class out here,' said Sara. 'Poor guy—his memory must really be going.'

'Just hope he doesn't remember he's put us through all this wind measuring stuff already,' Memphis told Sara quietly. 'Homework should be a cinch—we can copy it out of my—'

'Yes, I understand how the anemometer works, sir,' Vicki Starling said loudly. 'What I don't understand is how it ties in with the work we did last week on the South American rainforest?'

Sara saw Memphis cast a murderous look in Vicki's direction. 'Trust her!'

'What's that? Rainforests?' blustered Collier. He stared around him as if not quite sure where he was. 'Well, it doesn't tie in. Of course it doesn't.

What are you all doing out here, anyway? *Get back to the classroom!*' he roared with sudden fury. '*Right now!*'

Sara sighed and fell into line with the rest of her harried, bewildered classmates.

'Good going, Vicki,' Memphis muttered. 'You had to go and jolt Collier back to the real world.'

'Sorry.' Vicki shrugged and batted her perfect eyelids. 'But you wouldn't want our grades to suffer, would you?'

'No, not when there are more deserving candidates,' Sam muttered, miming strangulation, and Sara couldn't help but smile.

BReaTHeR

After forty minutes in the rainforest—or rather, a wonky cross-section of one on a noisy overhead projector—Sara was ready for Breather. When the end-of-period hooter finally gave its joyous honk, like a huge deranged goose waking up on Boxing Day with its neck in one piece, she couldn't pack her things away fast enough.

Collier rattled off a bit of homework for them, but Sara could tell his heart wasn't really in it— probably too embarrassed by his cock-up. He got up and walked stiffly through the door. Poor old duffer, why didn't he *want* to retire? Why would anyone *choose* to teach pains-in-the-bum like Sam and Smithy when they could be sitting at home watching TV?

'I think we should tell the Head about him,' she heard Vicki Starling saying primly as she headed for the door. 'Collier's got a screw loose.'

'Don't grass him up,' said Ruth Cook, to Sara's surprise. 'It's sad. My gran went funny like that. Ended up eating pot pourri and thinking it was crisps.'

'Plus we could get someone worse in his place,' Sam pointed out, and Ruth nodded vehemently. But Vicki and her mates simply walked out without another word.

Sara saw that Fido and Smithy were loitering by their desks with Sam, showing no signs of moving in a hurry. She and Memphis crossed to join them.

'What's up?' asked Sara. 'Trying to lose yourself in the rainforest canopy?'

Smithy looked at her. 'Do us a favour, Knotty. Look outside and check there's no runaway tea trolleys on the loose out there, yeah?'

'Or any mad caretakers with a bag full of mousetraps,' Fido added, shaking his reddened fingers.

'I'll go.' Sam was closer so he crossed to the doorway and took a look.

'Speaking of caretakers,' said Memphis. 'No time like the present for checking out the caretaker's hut for bits of handwriting.'

 57

Sara bit her lip. 'If he's mad now, what will he be like if he catches us breaking in?'

'Well, the man's here to work right?' said Smithy. 'Not sit in his hut all day. I say we check it out. You still got those notes, Memphis?'

'In my bag,' she told him.

'Hey, where did Sam go?' Fido wondered, and Sara realized that the doorway was empty. 'How do we know if the coast is clear?'

Apparently, it wasn't. For just a few moments later, Sam walked back inside with a rueful look on his face, and four gorgeous girls close behind him. Sara recognized the prettiest of them as Cassie Shaw from the year above; she was known to all as one of the hottest, most popular girls in the school. The tall, striking brunette beside her with the flushed cheeks was one of Cassie's mates, Marion Kind—which was lucky, since she was probably also Cassie's closest competition in the cute stakes.

'Guys, you won't believe this,' Sam croaked. 'God knows, I don't. But Cassie and her mates actually want to talk to you two!'

'To *us*?' drooled Smithy, his eyes almost on stalks.

 58

Fido had a sickening grin all over his face. 'W-what—what can we do for you ladies?'

Cassie folded her arms across her perfectly pressed shirt and looked at Smithy. 'You're Marcus Smythe?'

'Smithy to my friends.'

Cassie raised an eyebrow and turned to Fido. 'And you must be Dorian Tennant, right?'

'*Fido* Tennant,' he corrected her quickly. 'Never Dorian. I even make my mum and dad call me Fido.'

'I've got a better name for you,' said Marion. 'Pervert.'

'*Disgusting* pervert,' the girl next to her added.

'Peeping Tom,' said her mate.

From the look on Smithy's face, this wasn't quite how he'd pictured the conversation going. 'Er . . . did I miss something?'

'Well, if you did, I guess you can just play back your filthy, disgusting tape and see it again, can't you?' said Cassie.

'What?' Fido stared at her, baffled. 'What are you on about?'

'Hand it over,' Marion demanded. 'We want that tape!'

Sam frowned. 'What, you want it too?'

'Duh!' said Cassie. 'Like, we wouldn't!'

'But there's nothing filthy or disgusting about it,' said Sam.

'How can you *say* that?'

'It's just them having a laugh!'

One of the other girls rounded on Sam with fists clenched. 'You've seen it?'

'Yeah, I've seen it, so what? It's very funny.'

The girls looked almost affronted. '*Funny?*'

'It's hilarious,' Sam said brightly. 'Once Fido's edited the best bits together, they're bound to show it on TV.'

'TV?' Cassie squeaked. 'I don't believe I'm hearing this! Do you have, like, *any* shame?'

'Why should I be ashamed!' said Smithy crossly. 'It takes skill to do what I do—I'm a natural!'

The four girls stood open-mouthed and appalled.

'We're going to get you arrested,' said Marion.

'We're going to pound you into the ground,' swore the girl behind her.

Sara took an uncertain step forwards. 'You know, something tells me we might be talking at cross purposes. What do *you* think they've been taping?'

Cassie was almost trembling with rage. 'We just came from the sports hall. And we heard Mr Bruce on his mobile to some guy called Bill. And according to Bill, *Smithy* and *Fido* here sneaked a camcorder into the girls' changing rooms yesterday afternoon—and left it recording while we were getting ready for netball!'

Sara practically heard the boys' jaws dropping to the floor.

'What?' croaked Fido.

'We never!' gasped Smithy. 'I mean, we wouldn't dare!'

Marion grabbed Sam by the tie, half-choking him. '*This* one said he'd seen it!'

'No! I haven't seen anything like *that*!' Sam protested, gasping for breath. 'The tape's just of Smithy falling over! Stunt falls! Again and again!'

'Yeah, right,' said Cassie. 'That sounds likely.'

'It's true!' Smithy cried.

'So show us.'

'We can't,' said Fido, high-pitched and panicky. 'We haven't got the tape right now . . . Sara, *tell* them!'

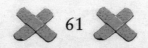

'I've heard enough of this rubbish,' said Marion. She lunged for Smithy, but with a yelp of alarm he ducked past her and ran for the door.

'After him!' yelled Cassie, and the other two girls dashed off in pursuit.

Sam and Fido looked at each other. Marion grabbed Sam by the arm, and Cassie lunged for Fido—but he was too quick for her and dodged out of the way. Unsure whether to help Cassie, Marion hesitated—and Sam pulled free. A moment later, he and Fido were pelting out of the door after Smithy.

'You can run but you can't hide!' Marion yelled after them. 'Peeping Toms!'

Now Cassie rounded on Sara. 'Are you two their friends?'

'Kind of,' said Sara carefully. 'Look, Sam was telling the truth. The only tape they've got is full of pathetic stunt falls. The closest it gets to the sort of tape you're talking about is when Connor Flint accidentally splits his trousers and shows the world a pair of crusty boxers.'

Cassie looked at her suspiciously. 'Maybe they just haven't shown you the changing rooms tape.'

'They wouldn't, would they?' said Marion. 'You're girls.'

'Well, why should you believe this bloke Bill that Brucie was talking to, anyway?' asked Memphis.

'Why would he make it up?' Cassie pouted. 'Anyway, Mr Bruce believed him. He said he would take the matter very seriously.'

'Must be a member of staff,' muttered Sara. 'Who else would have his number?'

'Well, look, ladies,' said Memphis reasonably. 'We've got Games with those boys next. When they show up we'll give them a real grilling, try and get them to crack.'

'Well, we're going to look for them too,' Cassie assured her. 'And when we find them . . .'

Sara sighed as the two girls stalked from the room. 'Poor old Sam—it's really nothing to do with him! So much for Innocent till proved guilty.'

Memphis looked at her. 'Do you think Fido and Smithy *did* do it?'

'Course they didn't!' Sara declared. 'I mean, apart from anything else, can you see Fido leaving his precious camcorder *anywhere*?'

'Good point,' said Memphis. 'Look, they left their bags here. Let's dump them in the cloaks on our way out.'

They walked from the classroom, stowed the boys' bags and left the humanities block to greet the warm, blowy day.

'I guess we should try to find the guys,' said Sara. 'If Cassie and her mates find them first . . .'

'Let's try the bike sheds,' Memphis suggested.

'Bit obvious, isn't it?'

'Still the best place to hide out. Plus we can look in on the caretaker's hut on the way. See if there are any handwriting samples lying around.'

'Oh great, yeah, let *us* be the ones who get caught!' Sara sighed.

But she went along with Memphis just the same.

'What's Biggins's first name?' Memphis wondered, as they passed the crash mats piled up at the side of the sports hall and turned off the pathway onto the grass.

'No idea,' Sara admitted.

'*Bill* Biggins, maybe? Could be *him* who called up Brucie about the changing rooms.'

'Why would he do that?'

'Trying to get Fido and Smithy in more trouble?'

'Maybe.' Sara bit her lip. 'But if Brucie's taking it seriously, he'll have to go and check out the tape in Steen's classroom. And when he does, he'll see that bit in the caretaker's hut where Biggins mouths off! So won't that plan rebound on our friendly neighbourhood bad-mouthed caretaker?'

'Maybe he's decided he won't be blackmailed,' said Memphis. 'He'll just get even.'

'Hey, speaking of guys with an interest in Fido and Smithy's tape . . .' Sara gestured to where two younger kids were standing a few metres ahead of them. 'Isn't that the guy who came over in Geography?'

'Linus Smellick,' Memphis recalled.

They were halfway across to the caretaker's hut by now. From here there was a good view of the bike sheds, and Sara could make out the incandescent acne of Connor Flint, loitering there with his gang. Linus and his mate—a skinny lad with big eyes and little freckles—were watching them from afar.

'Still gloating, huh?' she smiled. 'Has Connor patched up his trousers yet?'

'He's really mad,' said Linus solemnly. 'He'd do anything to get even with Fido and Smithy. Everyone heard him say so.'

Sara looked at Memphis. 'Another prime suspect for the phone call.'

The other boy tugged on Linus's sleeve. 'You going to introduce me or what?'

But Linus was frowning at Sara through his thick specs. 'Huh? What phone call?'

'Oh, nothing. You haven't seen Fido or Smithy around, have you?' she asked, quickly changing the subject. 'Or their mate Sam you spoke to?'

Linus shook his head.

'Well, at least that saves us walking all the way to the bike sheds,' said Memphis. 'Not that they'd be hanging with Connor, in any case.'

'*Excuse* me,' said the freckled kid sulkily. 'My name's Oscar, Oscar Donahue.'

'Hi and bye,' said Memphis, setting off again for Biggins's hut. 'Thanks for the warning, Linus. We'll pass it on to Fido and Smithy when we see them.'

'That is, unless Cassie Shaw and her hit squad have got to them first,' Sara added quietly.

'Hey! I heard everyone talking about it too!'

said Oscar, not wanting to be left out. 'That warning came from me too, OK?'

'Gotta run,' called Sara. 'Bye, guys.' She turned to Memphis. 'You heard what Linus said about Connor Flint wanting revenge. I'd say the Living Zit was more likely to spread a rumour about some pervy tape than anyone else—just to get back at Fido and Smithy. And of course, he couldn't give his real name—so he pretends to be this guy Bill.'

'How'd he get Brucie's number?'

'School office—bet they have a list of mobiles there. Even for the supply teachers.'

'I guess,' said Memphis. 'But as plans go, it's quite cunning. And cunning is not Connor Flint's style.'

'Judging by those stripy boxers,' Sara retorted, 'he doesn't have *any* style.'

They walked the rest of the way to the caretaker's hut in silence.

'Well,' said Memphis. 'Let's see if we can eliminate at least one of our motley suspects.'

Casually, they walked all round the hut, checking it was empty. They certainly couldn't *see* anyone through the single square window, and

 67

Sara's 'accidental' trip established that the only door was locked. But it also established something else.

'Look,' she breathed. 'This little name plaque . . .'

CARETAKER—W. E. BIGGINS

Memphis smiled. 'Could be W for William—Bill!' She crouched, pretended to tie her shoelace, while secretly lifting a corner of the doormat.

'No key,' she reported, disappointment in her voice. 'That's that then.'

'Biggins must have learned his lesson when Fido and Smithy got inside,' sighed Sara. 'Must be keeping the key on him at all times.'

'Who else would have one?' mused Memphis. 'I've seen Mrs Hurst come here before—I think some spare PE gear's stored inside.'

'That means Brucie might have inherited the key,' Sara realized. 'Maybe we could—' She tailed off as the hooter sounded for the end of Breather, jolting her back to her senses. 'Listen to me! I'm seriously thinking about nicking some keys so we can break into the caretaker's hut, all to prove some mad conspiracy theory!' She shook her head in disbelief, got up and started walking back towards the school. 'I'm turning into Sam!'

'Eeuuuw!' Memphis laughed, following her.

'It's true! We're so used to mad stuff happening around here, we just let ourselves get dragged along by it! Why?'

Memphis considered. 'Well . . . it's got to beat Games, right?'

'Ick.' Sara reflected for a few moments. 'You are *so* right. But, since I guess we have to go . . . maybe we can try fishing for a few answers direct from Mr Bruce while we're at it.'

'Sam would be proud of you,' said Memphis. 'Wherever he is.'

PERIODS FIVE AND SIX
GAMES

'We've looked all over, and there's no sign of them.'

'They've vanished.'

'Well, they can't hide from us for ever. And when the Head gets hold of that tape we'll make sure those nasty little creeps get suspended, expelled, *and* beaten to a pulp.'

Sam held his breath as the words of Cassie and her brutal buddies carried to him; not just from a heightened sense of tension, but because he had his nose wedged into Fido's armpit. After so much running about in the June heat, that pit was a bit on the ripe side.

Luckily, the girls had chosen not to investigate the neglected weather station too closely, nor the pile of old instruments discarded in the rain-trough. But then again, why would they? From the outside, there seemed barely room for one person in the low cupboard, let alone two—but in desperation, somehow, Sam and Fido had managed to fold themselves inside like cut-price contortionists.

Now Sam was clinging by his fingertips to the slats in the long, low cupboard's doors in case they gusted open in the warm breeze. When the rise and fall of the hooter signalled the end of Breather, both fugitives breathed a sigh of relief—once Sam had managed to extricate his nose from Fido's pit and jam it up against one of the slats.

'So they haven't found Smithy yet,' he hissed.

'Doesn't look that way.' Fido shifted awkwardly. 'Ouch. I think I'm sitting on a thermometer.'

'Don't need *that* to know the heat's on.' Sam's cramped, sweating limbs were buzzing with pins and needles but he didn't dare open the doors in case they were spotted and grassed up. 'You realize we can't go to Games now? You'd be dead meat—and thanks to Cassie and co., I'm guilty too, by association. Brucie would go mental at us.'

'He *might* believe us,' Fido argued weakly.

'And pigs might fly out of your butt.'

'Not while I'm sitting on this thermometer they won't. How long do we have to stay here?'

'Till we have a plan.' Sam sighed. 'Wonder where Smithy's holed up?'

'Wherever it is,' said Fido with feeling, 'it's got to be better than here.'

Putting off Games for as long as possible, Sara and Memphis popped into the girls' toilets in the nearby music block.

'I hate Cross Country,' moaned Sara, checking herself in the mirror. 'It's so boring.'

'At least we should be able to take a couple of short cuts,' said Memphis. 'Brucie won't be wise to them like Hurst is. We can hide out somewhere . . .'

'Knotty? Memphis? That you?'

Sara whirled round to find a pair of black shoes and dark trousers had become visible below the door of the last cubicle.

'Smithy?' she breathed.

Warily he opened the door. 'Who else would it be?'

'Duh—a girl?' scowled Sara. 'On the toilet, maybe?'

Smithy wrinkled up his nose. 'Gross!'

Memphis folded her arms and frowned. 'You know, if you're trying to shake the perv tag, this probably isn't the greatest hiding place you could go for.'

'The enemy never think to search in the heart of their own territory,' said Smithy smugly. 'Besides, smells better in here than in the boys' room.'

'So how long are you planning on hanging here?' said Sara. 'Till the end of term?'

'I haven't decided yet,' he said, and sighed. 'I just wish there was some way I could get hold of that tape.'

'To try and prove your innocence?'

'No, to make sure no teacher gets to it first and confiscates all those brilliant stunt falls!' He shook his head with frustration. 'I'm telling you, we'd get two hundred quid easy for some of those . . .'

'Someone's coming,' hissed Memphis. 'Listen, footsteps!'

'I think I need the toilet,' said Smithy, ducking back inside the cubicle. Then he popped back out. 'By the way, did you girls see what happened to my bag?'

'It's in the cloaks in the humanities block,' Sara hissed. 'Now get out of sight!'

Memphis walked out casually as if nothing was going on, but Sara couldn't stop herself from going up to the girl who'd entered.

'If I were you, I'd use a different loo,' she said, glancing back at the cubicle and lowering her voice. 'Someone's had an accident in here. *Several* accidents in fact.'

The girl frowned and went straight back out again, while Sara and Memphis swapped secret smiles.

But they didn't stay smiling for long. As they approached the sports hall, Sara saw Cassie and Marion waiting outside.

'Did you find those boys?' Cassie asked.

'No,' said Sara.

'And, like, we looked everywhere,' added Memphis, acting really cut up about it.

'They haven't shown up for Games yet,' said Marion. 'But when they do . . .'

''Ere!' Sara jumped as a familiar voice rasped out behind her. 'You girls should be getting on to your next lesson. Go on, hop it.'

It was Biggins. Swapping sour glances, Cassie and Marion turned smartly on their designer heels and strutted off.

'Sir, before we do,' said Memphis awkwardly. 'Could you tell us your name?'

Sara fought back a smile of astonished admiration. Memphis was going for it!

'My name?' He frowned at her. 'It's Biggins!'

'No, your first name, sir. You see, for History we're doing a survey of school staff names . . .'

He looked at her suspiciously. 'Why?'

'Er . . . we're comparing them to the names of people in school a hundred years ago and stuff,' said Sara quickly.

'The rubbish they teach you these days!' He shook his head wearily. 'Well, my name's Walter Edgar Biggins, if you must know. Just like my dad before me.'

Sara saw Memphis's face fall—then brighten. She took a pen from her bag and her rough book. 'You . . . er . . . you couldn't write it out for me, could you? Only I'm bad at spelling . . .'

 75

'Kids today,' Biggins grumbled as he did as he was asked. 'There. Now crack on to your next lesson—now!'

He bustled off on his way, and Sara and Memphis anxiously compared their two sets of handwriting.

'Not even close to a match,' sighed Memphis. She pointed to Biggins's scrawl. 'Looks like it was written by a constipated spider with four broken legs.'

'Plus Biggins is a Wally, not a Bill, which would seem to make him well and truly innocent.' She paused. 'Unless, of course, he's working *with* someone . . .'

The notion hung heavily in the air between them. Then Sara noticed guys from their class were starting to spill out of the sports hall in full kit. 'Come on, we'd better get changed. Don't want to upset Brucie.'

Memphis nodded. 'Wonder where he is . . . Watching the tape? Or back on the phone to his buddy Bill?'

Sam was still stuck for a proper plan of what to do next. The obvious answer was, throw open the cupboard doors and have a lovely big stretch. But he could still hear a few stragglers dawdling on their way to lessons, and he wasn't about to burst out of hiding in front of witnesses. Then again, if he and Fido sat here much longer in this sweltering, stifling heat they would either melt or fall to pieces.

'This is all so unfair!' said Fido morosely. 'Who would call up Brucie and tell him that rubbish about us taping the changing rooms?'

'This bloke Bill would, apparently,' Sam muttered. 'He's trying to drop you and Smithy right in it.'

'Yeah, but who is he, anyway? How would he even know what we were doing yesterday afternoon?' He wiped sweat from his eyes. 'Worst of all, why would he call me *Dorian*? The only people who call me Dorian are—'

'—teachers!' gasped Sam. 'Most of the *teachers* call you Dorian.'

Fido looked at him. 'You think Bill is a teacher?'

'Not just any teacher. A *supply* teacher,' said Sam triumphantly, as the facts finally clicked neatly into place. ' "Bill" is Janus. Mrs Janus, I *know* it!'

 77

'Janus?!'

'She called you Dorian this morning, and she called Smithy Marcus, right? And those are the names Cassie overheard Brucie repeating. It would explain why she called him up, too—she's bound to have her own brother's mobile number to hand, isn't she!'

Fido shook his head. 'But it was a *fella* who called up Bruce.'

'No it wasn't,' Sam told him patiently. 'Cassie only heard Brucie *say* the name, right? Well, get this—Memphis told me and Sara that Janus's first name is Belinda! So he could have been talking to *Bel*—not Bill at all!'

'I see what you mean,' whispered Fido. 'But—but why would Janus make up a rubbish story like that about the changing rooms?'

'We know how badly she wants to get hold of your camcorder—or the tape inside it.'

'Yeah, but Steen's already said he'll give her it at lunchtime . . .'

'I know. But obviously that's not good enough.' Sam took another deep breath of fresh air through the slats in the door. 'She must want it back sooner.'

'And so Janus tells her brother some made-up story about me and Smithy and a dodgy tape. Brucie gets all fired up and goes to get it straight away—and then she just taps him for the tape when he finds it's not dodgy after all.'

'But Steen's on a course this morning, remember?' said Sam. 'The camcorder is locked inside his classroom. How's Brucie going to get it?'

'If he thinks it's serious, Brucie could get Steen off his course and insist he hands over that tape! They could be on their way to collect it now . . .'

'Right. So *we* have to get there first.'

Fido looked puzzled. 'Why should we stop him? The sooner Brucie finds out there's no girls' changing room on the tape, the sooner the rumours will stop—and Cassie and her mates won't be out for our blood any more!'

'Don't be so sure!' Sam warned him. 'What's to stop people thinking you've got *another* tape somewhere? How can you and Smithy *ever* prove you're not guilty?'

'Er . . .' Fido wiped a bead of trickling sweat from his forehead. 'We can't.'

'Exactly. Only Janus can. She started the rumour

so she can get her hands on your camcorder—or more likely, on that tape we were watching this morning.'

'But why?' Fido sighed. '*Why* does Janus want that tape so badly?'

'There's just one explanation,' said Sam quietly. 'She saw something there in that footage that we all missed, and it left her well rattled.' He grinned. 'And I don't know about you, but I'm dying to know what it is! So—all we have to do is break into Softy Steen's classroom.'

'Why did I even get out of bed today?' groaned Fido. 'I should have pretended I was sick.'

'Well, I'm not going to pull out that thermometer you're sitting on to check your temperature.' Cautiously, Sam pushed open the cupboard door. The crowds had finally passed, snugly settling down to period five.

'Let's go,' he said.

'So *that's* Mr Bruce,' said Sara, as she and Memphis emerged from the changing rooms in their divine green and yellow kit. 'I can see the family resemblance!'

80

Brucie was stocky like his sister. He had the same big nose and the same strong chin. But he looked far less severe, despite having hair as short as a soldier's. He looked pensive—and it wasn't hard to guess what must be on his mind.

'All right, guys,' he told the assembled class, in a voice far softer than Janus's theatrical boom. 'It's cross country, so you'll go Mrs Hurst's usual way, boys and girls together—past the tennis courts, up the track, skirt past the woods, and down the far path for a circuit of the playing fields. Got it?'

'Got it all right,' Memphis murmured. 'Just don't want it.'

'But before we start . . .' Brucie scrutinized the little crowd. 'We've got people missing. Has anyone seen Dorian Tennant and Marcus Smythe?'

Sara and Memphis glanced at each other uneasily.

'Fido and Smithy?' Ashley shook his head. 'They were here in Geography.'

'Sam Innocent's not here, either,' said Vicki Starling. 'Maybe something's happened.'

 81

'Is it true someone's been filming the girls' changing rooms?' asked Ginger Mutton quietly, starting a wave of scandalized whispers. 'Only I heard Cassie Shaw say—'

'Oh yeah, Ginger's bezzy mate Cassie,' said Ruth Cook mockingly.

'I'm just saying what I heard,' Ginger protested.

'It's a rumour, that's all, and I'm sure there's nothing to it,' said Brucie. 'Even so, I'm going to get to the bottom of the matter.'

'Was that bottom caught on tape too, sir?' asked Ashley innocently, to much laughter from the boys. Clearly he'd spent too long sitting next to Sam in class.

Brucie ignored him. 'Now, you're sure none of you have seen these missing boys?'

Silence. Sara looked down at her shoes, trying not to blush.

And felt a sudden twinge of hope.

'Sir, my shoelace is broken!' she realized. 'Look! I can't run with a broken shoelace!'

Brucie sighed, shot her a glance. 'Does Mrs Hurst keep spares?'

'I don't know,' said Sara.

 82

'Well, go and look!' he said irritably. 'There might be some in the old kit box. The rest of you, get going. Girls first. I'll make a note of your start time . . .'

Sara ducked back inside. Normally Hurst left the old kit box in the communal area between changing rooms. Since it was nowhere to be seen, she guessed it must still be in Hurst's little office. She opened the door, and sure enough it was there beneath the desk.

After sorting half-heartedly through the ropy contents for a couple of minutes, she discovered to her dismay a total of three viable shoelaces. Then she heard footsteps outside, and muted conversation. Sounded like Brucie—and Softy Steen . . .

Sara crept over to the door, nervously threading the shoelace as she listened closely.

'Er . . . this is a bit uncool, Mr Bruce, to be honest,' said Steen. 'I'm only on a quick loo break, and I have to get back to my course. What's so secret?'

'This won't take long,' Brucie assured him. 'I just need the keys to your classroom.'

'Why?'

'It's a delicate matter.'

'Well, sorry, but I don't have them on me. I left them in the training room.'

'Can we go and get them now?'

'It's the other side of the school, I haven't got time. What's bugging you, anyway?'

Brucie took a deep breath. 'It's my sister . . .'

'Belinda?' Steen lowered his voice. 'I . . . er . . . noticed she's been acting kind of strange lately. Is everything all right?'

'Oh, yes, Bel's fine—well, a little overworked perhaps, but aren't we all, eh?'

Bel, thought Sara with an electric shock, as the identity of the mystery caller suddenly stood out like neon at midnight.

'Thing is,' Brucie went on, 'Bel's got a bee in her bonnet about a certain video camera tape . . .'

Now Steen sighed. 'I've already told her that I *need* that tape, at least until after lunch. I have some bigwig visitors coming this afternoon, to discuss taking my idea for a self-help club to other local schools—'

'Yes, well, I won't need it for long,' said Bruce. 'But you see, Mr Steen, it looks as if the tape

Tennant gave you could contain some very incriminating footage.'

'If it did, "Tennant" would hardly risk giving it to me, would he?'

'Nevertheless, I simply *must* check for myself!'

'Fine, you can have it in just a couple of hours!' Steen checked his watch worriedly. 'Now, I really have to get back . . .'

'Look, it'll take ten minutes to sort this matter out. Well, fifteen, I suppose, since you'll have to show me how to work the blessed camcorder—'

'I'm sorry but no way, OK?' Steen's voice was getting higher and going a bit wobbly. 'The Head's insisted I attend this training, we're getting close to an important bit—and then I must crack right on with editing that tape.'

Brucie gave him a nasty look. 'You've got a real attitude problem, mate.'

'*Me!*' Steen marvelled. 'You're a supply teacher, easy come, easy go. But I'm trying to build a career here. I need to raise my profile and if my club idea falls through—'

'Spare me the sob story.' Brucie's voice had hardened. 'Just be aware, this isn't over yet, Mr Steen. I fully intend to speak to the Head

 85

at lunchtime about your bullish behaviour.'

'Good!' Steen blustered. 'He'll probably be impressed with me! Now if you'll excuse me, I'd better . . .' He cleared his throat again. 'Mr Bruce, I'm *going* to get back to my course. Right away.'

'What *is* this training, anyway?' sneered Brucie.

'It's to make me more assertive!' Steen squeaked as he turned and bustled away. 'So there!'

'*Now* he gets assertive. Typical.' And with that, Brucie stomped off back outside.

'*Very* interesting,' Sara breathed, as she softly padded out after him.

The rest of the class had already set off on the run. 'Are you still here?' he snapped when he saw her.

She awkwardly tapped her newly repaired running shoe. 'I found a new lace.'

'Well, now it's on your boot, get on your bike!' he roared, with volume and ire worthy of his sister.

Sara set off at a gallop—but her thoughts were sprinting faster. So Janus was the mysterious Bill.

But what did she have to gain by involving her brother in her quest to get hold of that tape?

She forced herself to run faster, to try and catch Memphis up. She couldn't wait to spill the juice on what she'd just overheard. She only hoped her friend could make more sense of it than *she* could.

Slowly, stealthily, Sam led Fido through a flower bed towards Steen's classroom. He felt a bit like a commando—albeit a slightly rubbish commando with no special skills who didn't have a clue how he would complete his mission. Plus he had a rumbling stomach and his throat was parched.

'How are we supposed to get in?' complained Fido loudly. Still rubbing at the cramp in his arms and legs and plucking at the seat of his trousers, he was in a right mood. 'Smash a window? Break the door down? Ask a passing cat burglar to lend us a hand?'

Sam shushed him furiously. 'Speak a little more loudly, why don't you,' he hissed. 'I think there's probably someone in Norway who . . .'

 87

He tailed off. Fido glowered at him. 'Someone in Norway who what?'

'Who didn't hear Vicki Starling shouting this morning,' he breathed, suddenly excited. 'That Smithy, he's a genius!'

'He is?'

'Remember when he was mucking around being Vicki's dad this morning, just before Steen chucked him out? He was trying to open the window in case anyone hadn't heard his "daughter" yelling.'

'He's not *that* much of a genius,' Fido argued. 'He couldn't open it.'

'Yeah, but he fiddled with the catch, didn't he? Maybe we can force it open from the outside!'

'Guess it's worth a try.'

They swiftly cut across a walkway and into the last remaining bed of shrubs and bushes between them and the classroom. The vegetation was sparser here, so Sam started wriggling forwards on his belly like a marine under fire. But it was muddy and prickly, and besides, Fido was giving him funny looks. He joined him instead in a low, crouching crawl through the foliage.

'Was it this window?' Fido said uncertainly. There were three to choose from, and they'd gravitated towards the one in the middle.

Sam tried to cast his mind back. 'I dunno. I *think* so.' Sam reached up to the window, tried to prise his fingers under the bottom edge. It was stuck solid. 'Maybe if there was something we could wedge under it . . .'

Fido offered him a door key. Sam wrestled with the little wedge of metal, which was soon slippery with his sweat. He forced himself to be patient, wiping the key on his shirt each time he dropped it, working methodically at different points along the base of the window, ignoring the pins and needles in his protesting legs.

Finally, after twenty agonizing minutes of hard graft, the key scraped in between the window and the frame, allowing Sam to use it as a lever. With a crunch and some flaking paint, the window came free.

'Did it!' hissed Sam triumphantly.

Then he heard Fido clear his throat. He was kneeling a few metres to Sam's right—beneath another open window. 'It was *this* one, you pranny,' he hissed. 'I just tugged it and it swung wide open!'

Sam tossed him back his bent and battered

 89

door key. 'Doh! Or rather, wrong *win*-doh!'

Checking around to be sure there was no one coming, the boys took a window each and scrambled inside.

The classroom was quiet and cool after their exertions, but Sam was too pent-up to appreciate it. If they got caught now, he knew they'd be in *real* trouble . . .

Fido looked to be having trouble breathing. And then Sam saw why.

There was no sign of the camcorder on Steen's desk.

Sara had started running the cross-country route well, but about forty-five seconds later she'd decided enough was enough. Memphis was nowhere in sight, and clearly Sara would never catch her up, so there was just one thing to do—cheat.

She turned off the main path and on to the dirt track that led back to the school fields. If she was careful, she could just kick back and wait for Memphis to pass by later. She broke into a gentle jog.

'Careful, you'll wear yourself out going at that speed.'

Sara spun round—to find Memphis smiling out at her from the greenery at the side of the track. 'I figured you'd never run the distance,' she said. 'Like me, you've got too much sense!'

'But, you know, we're only cheating ourselves,' said Sara gravely. Then the two of them cracked up in hysterics.

'We'd better not stay here,' said Memphis, heading off down the track towards the playing fields. 'Hurst normally patrols down here to make sure no one's bunking. Brucie will probably do the same.'

'Speaking of Brucie,' said Sara, 'you won't believe what I've found out . . .'

Sara explained all she'd overheard as they made their way back. The playing fields extended all around the east side of the school and the sports hall, eventually leading on to the bike sheds and the caretaker's hut at the top of the school drive. The sheds, and the cover they afforded, were an obvious place to make for. They jogged along so they wouldn't look too suspicious, talking as they went.

 91

'So we have our Bill,' Memphis summed up. 'What we don't have is a motive.'

'Or a tape for much longer, by the sound of things,' sighed Sara. 'Unless super-assertive Steen gets pushed too far and takes on Bruce in a punch up.'

'I wouldn't fancy his chances,' said Memphis. 'Not against Brucie *or* his sister!'

'I wouldn't fancy his *career* chances either if he flunks this course and can't get his SHAPE idea off the ground,' said Sara. 'He's really worried about it, and Brucie was just horrible to him.'

'I heard some blokes in the year above saying Bruce was all right,' said Memphis. 'Must have been taking freak-out lessons from his sister—'

'Down!' said Sara, flattening herself against the ground. 'There's Brucie now!' His solid, stocky figure was striding over the same ground they'd covered at Breather, heading towards the hut and the bike sheds.

Memphis joined her in the grass. 'Well, what do you know. *He's* bunking off too!'

Sara frowned. 'And it looks like he's heading for the same hiding place as us.'

But Brucie stopped short of the bike sheds, veering away instead to Biggins's hut. Glancing about, he unlocked the door and stepped inside.

'What do you reckon he wants in there?' Memphis wondered.

'Must be Hurst's key,' Sara reasoned. 'Like you said, she keeps spare gear in there. But it stuffs up our plan to hide out in the bike sheds.'

'At least while he's busy in there, he won't see us sneaking back into school,' said Memphis, jumping to her feet quite athletically. 'You know, maybe we should hide out in the girls' cloaks— see if Smithy's still there, fill him in on what we know.'

'Be good to be out of sight for a while,' Sara agreed, looking around nervously. 'Let's go.'

Willing Brucie not to come out of the hut until they were safely past, Sara and Memphis started sprinting for safety.

'We're too late,' croaked Fido, staring at Steen's empty desk in the quiet of the classroom. 'The camcorder's gone. After all that effort—Brucie must have just walked in and taken it!'

93

Sam had a brainwave. 'Unless . . .'

He pulled open a drawer in the desk, cleared away some papers—then raised up his head and offered thanks.

The camcorder lay on its side at the back.

'Steen just didn't want to leave it out in plain view,' Sam said, grinning.

'Are you OK, sweetie?' Fido snatched hold of his silver baby and cooed to it. 'Daddy won't leave you again.'

'Stop mucking around and get on with it!'

Fido was already flicking the power on and opening up the screen. 'We were watching Smithy falling off the bike sheds when Janus came over, weren't we?'

Sam nodded. 'That was playing when me and Sara had to push off back to our places.'

The tape hummed as it rewound.

'You know,' said Sam, 'if Brucie *does* get his hands on this tape, he's going to see the stuff with Biggins. Maybe we should erase that while we're here.'

'It'll break Smithy's heart,' Fido sighed. 'But I guess you're right.' He stopped the tape, pressed play, and smiled. 'But not the footage with

Connor's boxers!' he said, showing Sam the little screen. 'They can't touch us for that—it was out of school hours!'

Sam chuckled again as Smithy went crashing and Connor Flint's gang went flying. Then he peered more closely. 'Hey, hang on. Isn't that Linus Thingie, the bloke who came up to us?'

'Looks like him.' Fido whizzed back to the start of the shot, and this time played it in slow-mo. They both looked together. 'Yeah, look—Connor's gang are just shoving him over when Smithy hits them like skittles!'

'No wonder Linus came up and thanked you!' grinned Sam. 'Serves them right. But come on, you'd better get back to yesterday lunchtime.'

They waited nervously as the camcorder buzzed backwards once more.

'Here we are,' said Fido, catching the start of the scene in the caretaker's hut and sighing. His hand paused over the record button. 'You really think I should—'

'Wipe it,' said Sam firmly. 'Then maybe you can make peace with Biggins. If you don't, he'll make your life hell for years!'

'Guess so,' said Fido, striking the button.

An uneasy minute passed as the incriminating footage was wiped for ever. The camcorder beeped shrilly as Fido paused it, making Sam jump.

'Now, let's get back to the stuff that bugged Janus so badly,' said Sam.

Fido whizzed backwards through the tape again. 'Here we go,' he said, finding the place and hitting play. 'Smithy on the roof, Smithy falling off the roof,' he narrated. 'Smithy climbing back on the roof again . . .'

Sam nodded as he peered over Fido's shoulder. 'Maybe Janus is just worried about Smithy hurting himself. I mean, it *is* kind of dangerous.'

'Oh yeah, it's dumb all right,' Fido admitted. 'But then she should just tell him off instead of going to all this . . .'

Both of them stared as, once Smithy had performed a particularly hair-raising fall, the camera wobbled and shifted away. Clearly, Fido had imagined he'd stopped recording. He hadn't. As he helped Smithy up, the camcorder pointed in a random direction—over at the caretaker's hut. There it stayed for a few seconds.

Through the glass of the hut window, there

was a sudden movement, a sparkle of light—the bling of a ring catching the sunlight.

'There's someone in the hut,' Sam realized. 'Look, there!'

But Fido had already seen. He paused the tape, fiddled with the picture settings, upped the brightness so they could see better.

The screen grew lighter, bit by bit. A familiar hairdo became apparent, like a big, coiling ring of poo on top of a fat round head. As Fido advanced the footage frame by frame, the figure turned around properly.

'It's Janus!' breathed Fido. 'What's she doing in the caretaker's hut?'

Sam cringed. 'Those are her bare shoulders! I don't think I want to see any more!'

'Sam,' said Fido gravely, 'we have to.' He set the tape going in slow-mo.

Frame by frame, Janus was pulling on a sweater over her head. Luckily for the contents of their stomachs, the rest of her was out of view. And then the camera wobbled and went dark as Fido pressed on the lens cap, obliterating the terrible image.

'She was putting her clothes on!' Sam croaked.

'In Biggins's hut! That can only mean one thing!'

'Holy . . .' Fido stared at Sam in revulsion and horror. 'She's having an affair with the school caretaker!'

By the time she'd reached the music block, Sara was feeling less guilty about bunking off. She felt she'd done more running about trying to skive than if she'd just run the cross country course in the first place.

'I've got to rest a minute,' she panted.

Memphis looked round carefully before going inside, coping with all this exercise as coolly as she coped with life. 'Coast is clear. Quick, let's get inside!'

The toilets were empty, Smithy's cubicle included. No great loss, Sara supposed. She'd have been too puffed out to tell him much anyway.

For a few minutes they did nothing but catch their breaths. Then Memphis checked her watch. 'Just less than thirty minutes till lunchtime,' she reported. 'We'll hang out here till it's almost time for the hooter, then sneak back and pretend we've just finished that last lap of the playing fields. Even if Brucie realizes we've cheated, I don't reckon he'll waste much time on us.'

'He'll be after that tape,' Sara agreed. She crossed to the marbled windows, opened one a little way and cautiously peeped out. As well as the wide pathway snaking past the block, the steep grassy slope leading up to the playing fields was visible. 'We should be able to see the runners coming back this way. Then we'll know when it's a safe bet to join them.'

'Good thinking,' said Memphis, crossing to join her. Then she swore. 'Look out, it's Biggins!'

Sara took a step back from the marbled window, crouched and peered through it again. Sure enough, there was Biggins with his distinctive blue coat and shiny pink bald patch, making his way along the path. When suddenly someone stopped him.

'Janus!' whispered Sara. 'Where'd she spring from?'

'And what is she up to with Biggins?' Memphis wondered.

The pair had turned so Janus had her back to them, and her broad shoulders hid the skinny

99

caretaker from view. She was bearing down on Biggins, but try as she might Sara couldn't hear what she was saying. She was speaking too softly—almost *seductively*. And now she was taking hold of his hand . . .

'What *is* this?' hissed Memphis, appalled.

Suddenly the pair parted, going in opposite directions. Biggins stared after Janus, red-faced, and gave her an awkward wave as she strutted back down the pathway and out of sight.

'I'm glad we didn't get here any later,' said Sara with some relief. 'Wouldn't fancy running into either of those two.'

'And especially not the two of them *together* . . .'

Sara looked up at Memphis. 'Yeah, they did seem a bit *too* together, didn't they?'

Memphis was smiling slyly. 'You said it yourself. OK, so Biggins didn't write the notes. But he could have been working with someone. He could've been doing *more* than just working with someone.'

'Janus . . . and Biggins . . .' Sara grimaced. 'A couple? But she's married!'

'And he's revolting.'

100

'And so is she!'

Sara and Memphis stared at each other in horror, then chorused as one:

'EEUWWWWW!'

'No wonder Janus has gone so far trying to get hold of this tape.' Sam was still staring in disbelief as Fido played back the tape for the third time. 'If you're not looking for it, you'd probably miss it—but there it is. *She* saw it—and she couldn't take the chance on anyone else seeing her in there!'

Fido nodded thoughtfully. 'She must have told Biggins straight away!'

'That's why Biggins got Smithy with his trolley,' said Sam. 'That's why he got a mousetrap from his storeroom and put it in your bag!'

'And why we got the threatening notes,' said Fido. 'Never mind Biggins's bad language. The two of them need this tape back because it's dynamite evidence of what they're getting up to.'

Sam pulled a face. 'Don't. I don't even want to *think* of what they're getting up to.'

'Me neither. Gross me out the door!' Fido

cringed and chuckled. 'In fact, gross me right out the door, down the corridor, out into reception, and down the school drive into the path of a—'

'Shh,' Sam hissed. 'Heard something outside.'

'What?'

'You're the one being grossed in that direction, you tell me!'

But by now it was obvious. The noise was footsteps, coming closer.

'Quick,' said Fido. 'Back out the windows!' He swung a leg over the frame and gasped with pain as he tried to squeeze through.

Heart racing, Sam dashed for the same window he'd come through earlier. But before he could even get a foot through, the door handle jumped as someone tried to get inside.

Sam looked back over his shoulder at the small panel of safety glass in the door . . .

And saw Smithy there, staring dumbly down at the door handle as he tugged on it again and again.

Fido was almost shaking with relief as he extricated his leg from the window beside Steen's desk and stamped over to the classroom door. 'Smithy, you muppet! It's locked! You saw Steen lock it!'

'Worth a try,' Smithy retorted. 'I mean, I saw *you* were inside.'

Sam gave a shaky sigh of relief. 'We got in through the window. What're you even doing here?'

'Same as you—wanted to get hold of that tape before anyone else did.'

'It's a good job we did,' said Fido. 'We were just watching back the footage—'

'Before you scared the shot out of us,' Sam added.

Smithy grinned. 'I saw you try to get out the window. Pathetic! What if I'd been Janus?'

'Then you'd have been dreaming of smooching Biggins, your fancy man,' said Fido.

Smithy stared. 'You what?'

'We've caught Janus changing in his hut! Come round to the window and we'll show you.'

'Be there in five,' Smithy hissed, and he rushed away.

Sam shook his head, his heart still pounding. 'We should get out of here while we can.'

'We need to figure out what to do with this tape first,' said Fido. 'It's *evidence*.'

'Yeah, but what *can* we do with it?'

Fido scowled. 'Not let Janus have it, for a start.'

'Maybe you should tell her we've found her out . . .'

'Try to blackmail her you mean? Grow up! I'm in enough trouble already!'

'I don't mean *really* blackmail her!' Sam protested. 'Just make her take back those lies she's told about you and Smithy taping the girls' changing rooms. Clear your names.'

Fido bit his lip. 'You think she would?'

'Well, she's gone to a lot of trouble to try to get hold of this tape one way or another . . .'

Suddenly, they heard more footsteps from outside, the heavy clicking of formidable heels coming their way.

'Uh-oh,' said Sam. 'Sounds like . . .'

'Janus! She's after the tape again!'

They scooted over to the windows. Fido carefully lowered the camcorder through the window for a soft landing. 'Well, she's not getting her hands on that so easily!'

'She's not getting us either,' vowed Sam.

He took a deep breath to make himself thinner and launched himself head-first through the gap

in the window. He felt the metal frame scrape against his stomach, heard a shirt button ping off as he scrambled through the opening. Heard a key rattle noisily in the door lock as he fell awkwardly to the ground with a thud. He started to move, but the foliage rustled at alarming volume. A moment later, as the door creaked open, Fido flopped through his own window and cracked his hip on his camcorder; luckily he managed to stifle his gasp of pain.

But like Sam, now he didn't dare move. The heels clicked across the room, closer, closer. He heard the desk drawer squeak as it was pulled roughly open . . .

This wasn't fair! They were only supposed to have Drama with Janus after lunch—not right through the day.

Sam knew she would soon find the camcorder missing. And both windows were still ajar—clear signs of trespass. If she so much as glanced out of them she would see them. And then they were in deepest, *deepest*—

Suddenly, something ricocheted off the far window—the only one still closed—with a clatter. Sam craned his neck to see where the noise came from, and saw Smithy, just visible from this angle in the flowerbed across the pathway, aiming another little pebble at the same window.

Sam grinned to himself. The guy really *was* a genius. He must have seen them outside and guessed from the way they were lying there that it wasn't safe to move—so now he was trying to draw Janus's attention to the *other* window.

There was the squeak of the drawer again, and the clicking of those heels. Sam signalled to Fido that this was their chance to get away. Fido nodded, and this time they moved off surely and swiftly on bellies and elbows like true commandos, wriggling for the safety of the nearby ivy and lavender bushes.

Through the fronds of green and lilac Sam saw Janus stare out suspiciously from the far window. But, seeing no one, she soon retreated from view—no doubt ready to tear the classroom apart to try and find the missing camcorder.

'Unlucky.' Sam smiled grimly to himself.

'Her or me?' Fido shook his head wearily. 'I just remembered. We've got the tape now, but

 106

we're meant to put it under the crash mats at the start of lunchtime, remember?'

Sam groaned. 'Oh God, I'd forgotten that.'

'If we don't . . . who knows what'll happen!'

'Fifteen minutes to go,' said Sam, checking his watch. 'Not long.'

'Let's hook up with Smithy,' said Fido. 'And try to work out what we do next . . .'

From the safety of the toilets, Sara had counted a few weary figures now, staggering towards the sports hall in their muddy kit.

'Five minutes till lunchtime,' Memphis announced. 'Reckon we can finish our run now.'

'Come on then,' said Sara nervously. 'But if we get away with it, let's not push our luck for a little while, huh?'

Memphis opened the door, checking the way was clear. 'Wonder what luck Brucie's had, trying to get hold of the tape?'

Hovering in the doorway to the music block, they watched the straggling athletes as they slithered down the steep grassy slope on to the concrete, waiting for a good gap. Then they ran to the base of the slope and joined in the race, puffing and panting quite convincingly over to the concourse outside the sports hall.

But their subterfuge was all in vain. Brucie wasn't even there.

'What happened to you two?' Ruth Cook was eyeing them suspiciously, her hair spiked up with sweat. 'Never saw you running.'

'We move like the wind,' said Sara quickly.

'While Ruth just smells like it,' Memphis muttered.

The concourse swiftly filled with sweaty athletes, milling about in confusion. Then Brucie finally reappeared on the scene. He was holding his left hand as if he'd hurt it, and looked totally miserable.

'Well done, you lot,' he said, forcing a small smile. 'You may not have seen me, but I was keeping tabs on you, of course. You all ran well.'

Memphis raised an eyebrow. 'What, you really think *I* did OK, sir?'

'Yeah,' he said, still clutching his fingers. 'Good effort. Now, in you all go now, shower and get changed. Come on, get going.'

'What did you do to your hand, sir?' Sara

 108

wondered as her classmates trooped wearily off to the changing rooms.

'I . . . er . . . sprained it lifting some stuff.' He clamped his hand around his fingers a little more tightly. 'It's nothing. Now get going.'

She shrugged and followed the crowd inside. Memphis was waiting for her.

'I don't believe him for a minute,' said Sara. Clearly, Brucie was hiding something. But what?

Lunchtime

For Sam, the hooter was a welcome signal that he could leave the toilets and mingle in a fresher-smelling world for a while. But from the look on Smithy's face, it might have been the tolling of a death knell. He kept clicking his tongue, fiddling with his fingers, his forehead furrowed with frown lines. Fido sat silently inside one of the cubicles; perhaps the pressure was getting to him in other ways.

'Well, guys,' Sam said gently. 'We can't stay in here for ever.'

'We can,' Smithy argued.

'Fantastic!' cried Fido suddenly from the cubicle.

'Well, all right, I suppose we can.' Sam waved a hand in front of his nose. 'But do you really *want* to?'

The three of them had grabbed their bags from

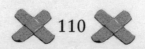

the cloaks and ducked in here for a council of war. Fido was quite tempted to keep hiding out till hometime in the hope they could remain undiscovered. But Sam knew that situations like these didn't blow over. They only blew up.

'It's a nightmare,' said Smithy simply. 'How did we get into this?'

'You fell into it, several times, in front of a camcorder,' Sam reminded him. 'Shame you didn't use a stuntman!'

Sam reckoned they should go out to the crash mats and face up to whoever had left the threatening notes. 'I'll go with the tape by myself if you like. Drop it under the crash mats and see who comes looking. Then, when the Head catches up with you, you can name a few names of your own.'

'Yeah, just before he expels us,' sighed Smithy.

There was a plaintive beep from the cubicle. It sounded like the camcorder. Was Fido actually *filming* in there? A few moments later he gave a satisfied chuckle.

'Let's wait outside,' said Sam worriedly, heading for the exit. 'I'll just check no one's lurking out here—'

'Oh, what's the use?' Smithy picked up his bag

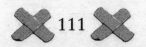

111

sulkily and pushed past him. 'Let's just go to the crash mats and get it over with. Take on whoever's doing this and show 'em we're not gonna be scared.'

'Take them on?' said Sam frowning. 'Not so fast with the *we*!'

Then Fido appeared behind them, eyes wide and shining and a big grin on his face. 'Guys! Like I said, it's fantastic! Check it out—you won't believe what I just did.'

'Mate,' said Smithy impatiently, 'if you're this excited about a bowel movement, I feel sorry for you.'

'Not that,' Fido groaned. 'Listen—'

'No more waiting, hiding, *or* listening,' said Smithy, ticking these unmentionables off on his fingers.

'How about running?' said Sam, pointing down the corridor.

Cassie Shaw, Marion Kind, and a whole platoon of vengeful-looking babes were marching down the corridor towards them.

'Get them!' Cassie cried.

Smithy and Fido whimpered as the girls broke into a small stampede.

112

'How about running really fast?' Sam prompted them. 'And hoping for a miracle?'

The three of them sped off through the crowded corridors.

'Where's a teacher when you need one?' gasped Fido as they burst out of the block and into the warm daylight.

'With our luck it'll be Janus or Brucie!' Smithy grunted.

But it seemed that luck was actually on their side. The path led to a crossroads outside the canteen, and Sam spied Memphis and Sara walking that way, no doubt heading off for their lunch.

'This way, guys,' he panted, veering off to intercept them. 'Move faster! We have to get out of Cassie's sight for this to work . . .'

'Where's the fire?' asked Memphis as they approached.

'We're gonna be slung on top of it if you don't help us out,' Sam panted.

'Lynch mob, huh?' Sara nodded wisely. 'Get in the bushes.'

Fido grinned. 'Wow, I never knew you cared!'

'Do it,' she scowled, grabbing him by the collar and shoving him into the nearby undergrowth after Sam and Smithy. Then she and Memphis stood guard in front.

Sam peeped through the stiff, leafy little branches. He held his breath as Cassie and her cronies hesitated at the crossroads in the path, looking all about. Then, as if following a scent, they headed for the canteen—and the boys' hiding place.

'We're so dead,' breathed Smithy.

'Hey, Cass,' called Memphis, stepping forward as the girls approached. 'Looking for the tape creeps, right? They went *that* way!'

She pointed right, in the direction of the science block and the school farm.

Cassie and co. nodded grimly, and set off again in pursuit—only this time it was wild geese they were chasing.

'Nice one, ladies,' said Smithy, rising up from the foliage.

'Now wait till you hear what we've found out,' Sara told him. 'Bill is actually—'

'Belinda Janus,' said Sam. 'Yeah, we figured that out.'

Sara looked disappointed. But she wasn't beaten yet.

 114

'*And* we saw Janus and Biggins together! It looked like—'

'They might be a couple?' Sam shrugged as if this was old news. 'Yeah, we got that too.'

'We got it on *tape*,' said Fido. 'That's what this is all about!'

'Fido and me got in to Steen's room through the window and checked the footage,' Sam explained.

Smithy nodded queasily. 'Seems we accidentally caught her putting her clothes back on in Biggins's hut!'

'Gross!' chorused Memphis and Sara, their eyes nearly popping out of their heads.

'So *that's* what sent Janus off into one,' said Sara.

Memphis grimaced. 'If she's cheating on her old man with a *really* old man, no wonder she's trying to keep it quiet!'

'Explains why Biggins threw that trolley at me,' said Smithy.

'And got me with the mousetrap,' added Fido, looking ruefully at his fingers.

'And sent the threatening notes to get the tape back,' Sam concluded.

 115

But Sara shook her head. 'The notes weren't in Biggins's writing. We checked.'

Sam shrugged. 'So he got someone else to write them.'

'I just can't believe Biggins would do that,' said Sara.

'A man capable of snogging Janus is capable of anything,' Memphis reminded her. 'I mean, ugh! She looks just like her brother!'

'Speaking of Brucie, he's probably at the Head's office right now,' said Sara. 'Steen wouldn't give him the tape so he's calling in the big guns. He really believes what his sister told him.'

'Won't do him any good,' said Sam. 'We took the camcorder and the tape.'

Sara raised her eyebrows. 'You *took* them?'

'Well, it *is* mine,' said Fido, producing it from his bag. 'Anyway, we had to—Janus came into the classroom to get it herself. Nearly caught us.'

'So can we see the gross bit of her changing?' asked Memphis gleefully.

'Sorry, not right now,' Fido began, ''cause I've—'

But Sam shushed him, trying to think. 'She

116

must have got the keys from Biggins—he must have keys to all the classrooms.'

'But that doesn't make sense,' Sara argued. 'If Biggins has the keys, why didn't *he* just unlock Steen's door at break and help himself to the tape—save him and her all this trouble?'

'Get back in the bushes, you lot!' hissed Memphis.

Sam and his mates dived back into the greenery without hesitation.

'Cassie again?' Fido whispered.

'Uh-uh. Steen and Brucie.'

Sam could hear their voices carry.

'What do you mean, the tape's *gone*?' Brucie demanded.

'I've searched the classroom from top to bottom,' said Steen miserably. 'And it's gone!'

'You're certain you didn't leave it somewhere?' asked Brucie.

'Positive. Someone must have taken it!' Steen sighed. 'I don't know what I'm going to tell Fido . . . And as for my meeting . . .'

'Come on, Steen, think assertive, remember? We'll get that tape back.'

'And the camcorder, too, I hope!'

 117

'Yes, quite. But we've *got* to find that tape. So come on! We'll search the whole school if we have to . . .'

As the voices faded, Sam stuck his head up out of the bushes and sighed. 'Well, I guess it's no surprise they've both flipped. Bet Janus will be doing her nut too.'

'Surprised she didn't go wailing up to Steen herself,' Sara agreed.

'If only we could tell him she was snooping around in there,' said Fido popping up into view, 'without giving ourselves away!'

'Speaking of giving ourselves away,' said Sam, 'if they find *you* with the camcorder, Fido, we're gonna be in serious bother!'

'And speaking of bother,' said Smithy looking nervously about, 'won't take Cassie long to realize we're not in the science block *or* the school farm. We need to get going. Crash mats?'

'Crash mats,' Sam agreed.

Fido nodded. 'Fine. And we'll leave the tape there if that's what they want.'

'What?' said Sam. 'Just hand it over on a—?'

'Shhh,' said Fido with a smile, getting his own

 118

back. Then he ran off, and Sam and Smithy had no choice but to follow.

'We'll come too,' said Sara.

'Keep a safe distance, then,' Sam told her. 'We may need you to lead off the enemy again!'

But he knew that today they had made so many enemies, no one could keep them off their backs for ever.

It wasn't long before the sports hall came into view. Sam's stomach tingled with anticipation. Who would they find waiting for them at the crash mats?

Smithy grabbed hold of Fido's shoulder, slowing him down. 'You sure about this, Fido?'

'Sure I'm sure,' said Fido. He brought out a little tape from his pocket. 'Here it is, ready to hand over.'

'I'll go first,' said Sam. 'Suss things out.'

He left the other two at the corner of the hall and walked casually out to inspect the crash mats, a raggedy pile of big, blue squashy slabs. No one was in sight—except for the boys' number one fan, Linus Smellick, hanging out with some scrawny freckled kid.

'All right?' said Linus, pushing his big glasses up his nose.

'Been better,' Sam admitted. 'Seen anyone hanging around here?'

'Nah. Just me and Oscar,' he said, nodding to the guy beside him. 'We often come here. Nice and quiet. Gets you out of people's way.'

Sam could guess *which* people, remembering the way Linus had been pushed around by Connor and his gang on the tape. 'Haven't seen Biggins anywhere then?'

'Biggins?' Linus screwed up his little snub nose. 'Nah. Where are your mates, anyway, with that video?'

'Funny you should mention that,' said Sam, glancing behind him. Fido and Smithy were peering out from around the corner of the hall. Seeing it was safe, they came over to join him.

'All right?' smiled Linus.

'Surviving,' said Fido, staring down at the little tape in his hand.

'Not for long.' The younger boy's smile twisted into a leer. 'Here you go!' he shouted at the crash mats. 'I said I'd bring them right to you—*with* the tape on them. Now you can mash 'em to pieces!'

Sam stared in alarm as, like zombies rising from the grave, a parade of tough-looking blokes straightened up and stepped out from their squashy blue cover. They quickly fanned out to surround Sam and his mates in a loose circle, to cut off their retreat. And the biggest of the boys, his ugly face livid red with anger and acne, was Connor Flint.

'It's an ambush!' squeaked Smithy, as Fido discreetly slipped the tape into his bag.

Sam rounded on Linus. 'And *you* led us into it!'

'Uh-huh,' Linus boasted. '*I* was the one who shoved the tea trolley at Smithy!'

'But I was the one who told you to,' chimed Oscar.

'*And* I put the mousetrap in Fido's bag.'

'But *I* was the one who found it in the storeroom!'

'And I tricked you good. I made you think I thought you were cool.' Linus turned triumphantly to Connor. 'I told you it would work! You can count on me. I *told* you I'd get results!'

121

'But why?' Sam demanded. 'He was shoving you around this morning!'

'He shoved me around too!' said Oscar indignantly. 'He shoved me loads more!'

'He never!' insisted Linus.

'I dealt with the both of them,' Connor agreed, baring broken teeth in a cruel smile. 'Cheeky little shrimps were begging to be in my gang. Reckoned they were hard enough to hang with the big boys. As if!'

'We told him to push off,' said one of Connor's mates.

'Just before doofus here rode his bike into us,' growled another.

'You said we had to earn our place,' whined Linus. 'Well, we have! We've delivered them here, to a nice quiet spot for you to deal with them—*and* got you the tape back.'

Connor stared at Smithy and Fido. 'I was just gonna do you over, see. But four-eyes here persuaded me to wait. If you never showed, I'd have done him over as well.'

'And me!' said Oscar automatically. 'You'd have *really* done me over!'

'Shut it,' Connor snarled.

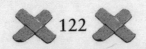

'So much for your biggest fan,' said Sam, turning to Fido and Smithy. 'He was Connor's groupie all along, stitching you up.' He rounded on Linus. 'You were in Collier's class first thing, weren't you? He took you all out to the weather station—and you and Oscar here didn't bother going back.'

'When we saw Smithy all alone in the corridor, we hid out in the storeroom while we planned how to get him,' said Linus smugly. 'Collier's so barking these days, he never even noticed us missing.'

'So you trashed the storeroom looking for something to use against Smithy,' Fido realized.

'Yup.' Linus nodded. 'When we found the mousetrap we were going to use it on Smithy. But when Biggins came by with his trolley and slipped off to the cloaks, the opportunity was too good to miss!'

'And you gave the mousetrap to me instead,' said Fido. 'Thanks.'

'And now *you* can give *me* the tape,' said Connor, shoving Oscar and Linus aside. 'Right now.'

'Sorry, seem to have lost it,' said Fido quickly.

'It's in his bag!' cried Linus. 'I saw him put it in.'

One of Connor's heavies snatched the ruck-sack from Fido's hand.

'Hey!' Fido snapped.

'Want it back, do you? Wanna fight me for it?' Connor reached into the bag, pulled out the little tape—and then the camcorder. Again, he gave his frightening smile. 'Well, well. Looks like I've got me a bonus.'

'Get your hands off that!' cried Fido.

'No.' He tossed the sleek little camcorder in one hand. 'Finders keepers. I'm nicking it. I can tape myself beating you up and give copies to all my mates.'

Fido finally snapped. 'Give me that back *now*, pizza face!'

Oscar and Linus gasped. Even Connor's thug squad couldn't help but flinch.

Sam swore he could see the pustules swelling on Connor's cheeks as he fixed Fido with cold, pale eyes. '*What* did you call me?'

Fido's concern for his camcorder had blinded him to caution. 'Pizza face,' he repeated angrily. 'Which in your case is short for *roadkill* pizza face.'

Connor was glaring in utter disbelief, curling his fists.

But Fido wasn't through yet. 'Which is *actually* short for roadkill pizza which someone burnt in the oven, dropped on a filthy carpet and stamped on—'

'OK, that'll probably do,' Sam interrupted.

'—before adding rancid pus and, like, loads of really ugly scars and scabs—'

'Gotta be moving along now!' grinned Sam weakly.

'—*face*!' spat Fido.

For a stunned moment, no one moved.

Then Connor and his gang started to close in on Fido, Sam, and Smithy.

Just as Cassie Shaw and her girlie hit squad appeared from round the corner of the sports hall like the Seventh Cavalry—led by *Memphis* of all people.

'There they are, Cassie!' she yelled. 'And look, Connor Flint's got the tape!'

'Get them!' Cassie bellowed. '*All* of them!'

Suddenly a fair-sized portion of hell broke loose—with perhaps just the tiniest pinch of heaven, as Connor Flint disappeared under a

gaggle of girls. Sam ducked behind one of the mats and surveyed the carnage in confusion. Members of Flint's gang were struggling to get away but the ruthless females showed them no quarter. Linus burst into tears as Marion Kind sat on him, while Oscar kept running up to random girls, crying, 'Pick on me! I'm here too! Pick on me!'

Then the inevitable happened and Sam felt arms pincer round his waist. He started to struggle, but the vice-like grip held him tight.

'Ouch!' he yelled. 'Leave me alone!'

'How feeble are you?' hissed a voice in his ear. 'You could at least try to fight back!'

It was Sara.

'I . . . er—I knew it was you all along,' Sam said quickly. 'Didn't want to hurt you.'

'Yeah, right.'

'Thought you were meant to be getting Cassie's lot off our backs? You led them right to us!'

'Looked like you needed a distraction,' she hissed. 'Now pretend to struggle.'

'Why? I'm quite enjoying it.'

'Yeah?' She squeezed tighter, nearly cracking his ribs. 'Just be good and play along. I'll try to get you clear. We saw Steen and Brucie were

126

heading this way—think it's best if we avoid them, don't you?'

'What about the others?'

'Memphis has got Smithy, she'll—'

'She hasn't, you know.' Sam pointed.

Oscar had grabbed hold of Memphis's shirt and was tugging her like an overgrown terrier through the sprawling, struggling bodies. 'Beat me up!' he begged her. 'Come on! If Linus can take it, I can!'

'Help!' yelled Smithy. 'Somebody help!' For the first time in his life, he had a girl on each arm. Unfortunately, they happened to be holding him in a full nelson.

'My camcorder!' gasped Fido, as Cassie Shaw gripped him in a necklock. 'I've got to get it back! Do what you like to me but don't let him hurt my camcorder!'

'*What is the meaning of this?*'

The rumbling bellow was worthy of Mrs Janus herself, and for a moment Sam thought she'd arrived on the scene. But as he and Sara sprang apart, he could tell by the family resemblance that Mr Bruce had turned up—with Softy Steen right behind him.

 127

'Too late,' breathed Sara. 'They found us.'

A dreadful hush fell over the battlefield.

'Well?' Bruce roared.

A burly girl was sitting astride Connor. Now she held tape and camcorder triumphantly aloft. 'We wanted these!'

'They filmed us in the changing rooms!' cried Cassie Shaw, reluctantly loosening her grip on Fido's neck. The rest of her private army mumbled their agreement. 'We all know it!'

'We know no such thing,' said Brucie firmly. He picked his way through the bodies to get to her, then snatched both tape and camcorder from her trembling grip. 'I shall view back this tape myself. Then *I* shall decide what action is appropriate.'

'That camcorder was stolen from *my* classroom, Mr Bruce,' said Steen, wringing his hands in agitation.

'That's not important,' said Brucie. 'We have it back now, don't we?'

'Now wait a minute!' Steen cleared his throat; tried to look really, really cross. 'Someone here took it. Who?'

'Please, sir, Connor Flint had it,' said Marion

128

Kind, removing herself from the sobbing lump that was Linus Smellick.

Connor struggled up in a daze, dabbing at one or two spots that had exploded in the struggle. 'Huh?'

'Yeah, that's true, he did have it,' said Smithy, clearly spying a golden opportunity. 'Everyone saw him with it, right?'

The girls nodded. 'He was holding it when we got here,' Sara said truthfully.

'We wondered how he got it,' said Smithy. '*He* must have broken into your classroom, sir.'

Connor's face was flushing again. 'I never!'

'No, he never! He nicked it off *that* kid,' said an especially thick member of his gang, pointing at Fido.

'I—I . . .' Connor glared at him and tried again. 'I was just . . . holding it for him.' In desperation, he looked to Linus for support, but the boy was still too busy weeping to contribute.

'See, me and Fido were trying to get the camcorder back for you, sir,' said Smithy earnestly.

'That's right, sir,' Fido chipped in. 'We knew you needed it ahead of your big meeting this afternoon.'

 129

'Mr Bruce, I think you should take this boy Connor to the headmaster's office,' said Steen.

'Not now,' said Brucie, clutching the camcorder as if it was a silver trophy. 'I tried him just as lunchtime started. He's in with Mr Collier and he won't be disturbed. So, if you'll excuse me . . .'

'But—but—' Steen spluttered, '*someone's* got to take control of this situation!'

'You're the one who's been on the assertive-ness course,' said Brucie briskly, turning the camcorder in his hands, as if stymied by its myriad buttons.

Steen stared at him, open-mouthed. Then he surveyed the throng before him, a slightly pathetic look on his face, his yellow flares flapping forlornly in the breeze. Connor and his gang were smirking, starting to mooch away, as if it wasn't worth hanging around. The girls were looking sulkily at Steen. If he didn't say something in a minute, they'd probably walk off after Connor.

Then suddenly he straightened up and clapped his hands together. 'Nobody move!' he roared in a very un-Steenlike fashion.

Jaws dropped left, right, and centre, and

130

Connor and his henchmen froze. Even Brucie looked over in surprise.

'I don't know exactly what's been happening here, and I don't exactly care!' Steen shouted. 'But I will not tolerate fighting in school of any kind. Line up in front of me, single file—now!' The fallen fighters scrambled up to obey. Steen stared around, a silly smile creeping on to his face. 'Now, guys, I'm going to take the names of everyone here and discuss your behaviour with your form teachers. *And* despite Mr Bruce's lack of enthusiasm, we're going to pay a visit to the Head. So let's have you! Make an orderly queue in front of me!'

Brucie started to walk away.

'Don't go far with that camcorder, Mr Bruce,' he barked. 'It's vital I edit that tape ahead of my meeting this afternoon.'

'Won't take me long to deal with this now. I'll bring it back.' Brucie gave him a tight smile. 'Besides, looks as if you'll be tied up here for a while, doesn't it?'

Sam watched forlornly as the incriminating tape was taken away.

'All right then,' said Steen, glaring at the line of red-faced pupils.

131

'Sir, you know *our* names, don't you,' said Sara, gesturing to her little group. 'So please could we be excused for now?'

'You were all involved in the fighting, too, and I can't let you off the hook,' he sighed. 'OK, guys. Go on ahead to the Head's office and wait for us there.' He looked at Fido and Smithy. 'And if Mr Bruce *does* find anything on that tape . . .'

'He won't, sir,' said Fido.

'Well, we'll see.'

Sam trudged off with Memphis and Sara ahead of Fido and Smithy, who were making obscene gestures at Connor Flint and Linus behind Steen's back.

'What about me?' objected Oscar. 'Don't just leave! Wave your fingers at *me*!' Then Connor thoughtfully elbowed him in the stomach, attention which probably cheered him up no end.

'Well, that was a total mess,' sighed Sam.

'Could've been worse,' Sara said tentatively.

'Like, how?' sighed Smithy.

Fido shrugged. 'At least I know my camcorder's safe now. Well, safer than if Connor still had it, anyway.'

'Oh yeah, great, t'riffic,' Smithy snorted. 'But on the other hand, we've lost the tape! We've stitched up Connor so he's *really* gonna be out for blood now. We've got to see the Head. And worst of all, Janus and Biggins have got the better of us! They've got back the evidence!'

'Actually, it's not *quite* as bad as you might think,' said Fido slyly. 'When I was in the toilet, I made an incredible discovery.'

Sara gave him a worried look. 'I'm not sure I want to know about this.'

Fido turned to Smithy and grinned. 'See, if you'd let me speak before, outside the Gents, instead of jumping down my throat, you'd have spared yourself this agony.'

Sam and Smithy stared at him. 'Well?'

'Back in the weather station cupboard, Sam— remember I thought I was sitting on a thermometer? Well, I wasn't. I was sitting on the spare blank tape I thought I'd packed!' Fido was all smiles as he produced a small plastic box from his pocket.

'But you turned your bag inside out looking for that before period one,' said Smithy. 'I saw you.'

'Stupid thing wasn't *in* my bag. I was in a real rush to leave the house this morning and meet up with you, and I must have stuffed it in the back pocket of my trousers.' He faltered slightly here. 'Or rather, *thought* I'd stuffed it there. But I must have shoved it down the waistband of my pants!'

'Ugh!' said Memphis.

Sara pulled a face. 'You're joking, right?'

'Stupid thing's been slowly working its way down,' Fido confessed sheepishly. 'I thought something was a bit itchy down there . . . But it was only when I went to the loo that I realized—there it was!'

'Like you'd laid an egg!' laughed Sam.

'Doesn't change anything,' grumped Smithy. 'What good is a blank tape to us?'

Fido opened up the little box to reveal the tape nestling snugly inside. 'It's going to be even less use to Brucie and Steen.'

Sara stared at him, her lips starting to curl upwards in a smile. 'You mean . . .'

'I switched them! I took out *our* tape in the toilet,' grinned Fido. 'I was just about prepared to leave a blank tape under the crash mats, but the real thing? No way!'

'Then we've still got all the footage!' Sam punched the air, all smiles. 'I'd love to see the look on Brucie's face when he realizes there's nothing on that tape.'

'Janus will go ape,' said Memphis gleefully. 'That was a slick move, Fido, I've got to hand it to you.'

'Hand,' Sara echoed suddenly. The others stared at her. 'Brucie's hand, I mean. Memphis, at the end of Games he said he sprained it, remember? He was holding it with his good hand like he was in agony. But you saw him just now—he was gripping that camcorder like there was nothing wrong at all.'

Memphis shrugged. 'Guess the hand got better.'

'Guess,' agreed Sara distantly.

Sam frowned at her. 'Well, what else? You think he was faking a dodgy hand? Why would he do that?'

'I don't know,' she confessed. 'Sorry. You're right.'

'Who cares, anyway,' said Smithy as he opened the door to the admin block. 'We're still in deep dog-mess. What are we going to tell the

Head? Everyone thinks we're peeping Toms!'

'And if he finds out it was us who broke into the classroom, we'll seem even guiltier,' sighed Fido. 'Like we were trying to destroy the evidence!'

'And if Connor gets the blame, he's *really* going to kill you,' said Sara cheerily.

'Like he wasn't before.' Smithy glared at Fido. 'I *told* you picking on him for a stunt was a bad idea.'

'You did not!' Fido protested. 'You said he was all mouth no trousers.'

'I was wrong,' Smithy sighed. 'He's all mouth, ripped trousers, stripy boxers, and big fists!'

Lunchtime was more than half over and the headmaster was *still* in his meeting with Killer Collier. Slumped with her friends in the reception room outside his office, Sara wondered if Vicki Starling had grassed the old codger up about his weather station mix-up. It was weird to think of Collier on the receiving end of a telling off . . . and she guessed the Head wouldn't enjoy the experience much either. So that would put him in a really good mood. Oh, joy.

She glanced at Sam, who gave her a cool little smile. Getting done was water off a duck's back for him, she supposed, he saw it as part of the job of being class clown—and Smithy was no stranger to finding himself in hot water. But Memphis and Fido were as quiet as she was at the prospect of a rap on the knuckles from the Head.

Knuckles . . .

An image of Brucie clutching his left hand flashed into her head. Then the sight of him holding the camcorder. Not a mark. Not a bruise or a swelling. So why . . . ? She had a sense that things were actually weirder than they seemed— even by Freekham High standards. As if she was missing something glaringly obvious in this whole situation.

Suddenly Steen walked into the reception area. He didn't look happy—and neither did the veterans of the crash mat scrap, queuing up behind him. Sara felt tense and self-conscious as they entered in silence, filling up the space, sharing chairs or crouching on the floor. Connor Flint fixed her with a livid stare that swept on to Fido, Smithy, and Sam in turn, but Linus, Cassie, and the others were apparently too cowed—or too bored—to summon much reaction.

'I can't believe the Head's not out of his meeting by now,' sighed Steen.

'His assistant said he mustn't be disturbed,' said Sam. 'Shame.'

'What's more of a shame,' said Steen, lowering his voice and turning to Fido, 'is that the tape confiscated from Connor Flint was a blank.'

Fido boggled. 'It was?'

Nice acting, thought Sara. Right now she knew the real tape was stuffed up his sleeve.

'It didn't take Mr Bruce long to find out,' Steen continued. 'He came running straight back, somewhat . . . er . . . frustrated.'

Sam, Smithy, and Fido kept their faces carefully neutral.

Steen looked at them sternly at first, then with a twitch of desperation. 'You don't know where the real tape is, do you?'

Smithy, Sam, and Fido shook their heads in uncanny unison.

'Oh well,' he said sadly. 'Mr Bruce is out searching around the crash mats in case someone dropped it in all the confusion. Perhaps he'll

have some luck.' He sighed again. 'I thought I'd get this lot a short, sharp shock from the Head, then go off and do my editing. Now it looks like . . .' He shook his head sadly and wandered away, his hands shoved deep in the pockets of his yellow flares.

Sara felt bad for him, even though he was a teacher. She remembered his conversation with Brucie in Games . . . No tape meant nothing to show his bigwig visitors, and no chance to make his mark. From the look on Fido's face, he was feeling kind of guilty.

And from the look on Connor Flint's face, he was feeling incredibly mad and was itching to do something about it. He kept switching his gaze between Fido and Smithy, his eyes hard and unblinking, as the long, sweaty minutes inched by.

After ten minutes and only the occasional thump and raised voice from the headmaster's office, Steen finally lost patience.

'There's only ten minutes left till afternoon registration,' he burst out, exasperated. 'And then only half an hour till my visitors arrive!'

But arriving ahead of them was Mrs Janus.

 139

She clopped in on her heels, turning a beady eye around the reception area.

'Still waiting to be seen, Mr Steen?' she enquired icily. 'And my brother tells me you *still* don't know what these people have done with the tape.'

'We haven't done anything with the tape!' Smithy protested. From the look of outrage on his face he was clearly a better actor than she'd ever been.

'Nonsense,' said Janus. '*And* disrespectful. I wouldn't stand for it if I were you, Mr Steen.'

Steen distractedly ran his hand through his hair. 'Please, Mrs Janus, I'm handling this affair in my own way.'

Sara watched the old trout's eyes at the mention of the word 'affair'—not a flicker. Maybe she *was* the better actor, after all.

'The Head will get the truth out of them!'

'Mrs Janus, the Head doesn't want to be disturbed!'

'I'm sure he'll spare us five minutes when he knows how important this is.' Janus knocked on the Head's door and opened it without waiting for an answer.

From where she was sitting, Sara had a ring-side seat.

Collier and the Head were busy talking over each other, but both broke off in mid-sentence at the interruption.

Janus was all smiles: 'I'm so sorry to interrupt . . .'

'Then don't, madam!' Collier complained.

'Not now, Mrs Janus,' the Head said tersely. 'I am in the middle of a very delicate discussion.'

'No, you're not, Ronald,' said Collier with sudden, stately calm, uncrumpling himself from a chair and dusting down his navy pinstripes.

'Oh?'

'It's over, and you win,' Collier declared with dignity. 'I'll retire as you ask, at the end of the term.'

A collective gasp went up around the reception. Even Connor Flint looked shellshocked.

'He gave in,' murmured Memphis. 'He finally gave in!'

Collier shuffled out and peered round at the full reception. 'Seems I've been holding everybody up for far too long,' he said sadly. Then his eyes seemed to focus on Linus and Oscar.

'Ah, Smellick, Donahue, there you are. I observed your absence from the end of my lesson this morning.'

Linus gulped. 'You . . . you did?'

'Indeed I did, most certainly. So you will report to my classroom after school for a detention. I shall see you both then.' He looked back into the Head's office and gave a whiskery chuckle. 'Well, if I have to go, Ronald, I'm going to damn well enjoy myself while I can!'

Sara smiled to herself. Once a killer, always a killer.

As Collier shambled off, the Head seemed to slump for a few seconds. Then he rose wearily from his desk, looking as if he'd just gone twelve rounds with a bull elephant. Mrs Janus opened her mouth, but he waved her into silence.

'I believe Mr Steen was here first,' he said, pinching the bridge of his nose. 'I'm sorry to keep you waiting for so long. How was the course . . . ?' He looked round at the packed reception in undisguised dismay. 'Oh. What would you have me do with this lot?'

'Erm . . .' Steen suddenly straightened. 'You know what, sir? Nothing at all.'

142

Janus turned the evil eye on him. 'What?'

'Mrs Janus wanted to see you on a related matter,' said Steen calmly. 'But I . . . I believe I can handle it myself.'

'Excellent, Mr Steen,' beamed the Head. 'I believe you can handle it too. In which case, I'll take advantage of the last minutes of lunchtime to eat my sandwiches.'

Sam scratched his head, looking totally baffled. 'Am I dreaming all this?'

The Head retreated back into his office. 'Come and see me later, Mr Steen, and you can tell me all about it. Oh, and good luck in your meeting!'

The door closed behind him.

For a few seconds, Janus stood speechless. Then she stormed away, muttering furiously under her breath.

'Her Drama class this afternoon is going to be *real* fun,' sighed Memphis.

Sara eyed Steen warily. Clearly he'd finished his training with flying colours, going from a wannabe-cool softy to assertive in seconds.

'You'll all report to my classroom for detention tomorrow lunchtime for causing an affray,' Steen announced to his prisoners of war. 'I'll inform your form teachers of the reasons why. Oh, and Connor, you'll come and see me every day next week so we can discuss why taking people's property is not acceptable.'

'But, sir—'

'No buts, Connor—except *your* butt parked daily on a chair in my room.' He surveyed the crowded reception. 'Well, I suppose that's about it until this controversial tape turns up. You can all go.'

With a mixture of relief and resentment, the surly gaggle of captives slouched away.

'Sir,' said Fido, rubbing his sweaty palms on his trousers. 'You really need that tape, don't you. For your meeting?'

Steen shrugged. 'I'll think up something to tell my VIPs.'

'Well, you know, I've been thinking about it . . . Maybe I do know where that missing tape might be . . .'

Sara, Sam, and Smithy gave him a synchronized frown. Memphis—laid back as ever—merely arched an enquiring eyebrow.

Steen was watching him carefully. 'Oh?'

'There's a litter bin near the sports hall—some-

144

one might have chucked the tape in there. Maybe we could go check?' He shrugged. 'If we find it fast, you might *just* have time to do the editing.'

'I might,' Steen conceded. 'All right, Fido. Let's join Mr Bruce in his search.' They set off down the corridor together. 'But if you think this means you're getting out of detention tomorrow . . .'

'Thought never crossed my mind, sir.' Behind his back, Fido wriggled his arm so the tape dropped down his sleeve and into his hand. 'I just hope I can find it for you . . .'

Smithy stared after them in disbelief. 'What's he playing at? If he helps out Steen he'll drop us right in it.'

'Then again, *someone* needs to see that tape to know that this footage of the girls' changing rooms doesn't exist,' said Sam. 'And like we just saw, the Head actually listens to Steen!'

Sara nodded in agreement. 'And let's face it, he's the one you need to convince.'

'But we can't prove we haven't got another tape of the girls' changing rooms somewhere,' said Smithy. 'And if Steen or the Head see that stunt we shot in Biggins's hut we'll get totally done!'

'We wiped it already,' Sam assured him. 'But not the bit with *Janus* in the hut. Once people see that, it'll be obvious she's been up to something with Biggins—and just as obvious why she's got it in for Fido and Smithy, for catching her on tape!'

'*And* why it suited her to make up the rumour about us and the changing room!' grinned Smithy. 'I like it!'

'Let's just hope Brucie doesn't barge in and get hold of it first,' said Memphis. She looked at Sara. 'You're quiet. Everything OK?'

'Yeah, I'm fine,' she said. But her thoughts were still chasing their tails. Something wasn't right . . .

Come to think of it, was *anything* right? Steen taking charge . . . Collier walking out . . .

The world's gone mad, Sara thought. This had to be the weirdest Freekham day ever.

And it wasn't over yet.

Afternoon Registration

The last seconds of lunchtime liberty were overthrown by the remorseless honk of the hooter. The boxy, modern buildings of the school soon drew everyone back inside like evil magnets.

Word of Collier's shock retirement move had spread faster than chicken pox. As Sara and her mates weaved their way through the science block, they caught snatches of gossipy conversation.

'Good riddance to the old . . .'

'Reckon he'll get a medal for two hundred years of service?'

'You've heard of the ravens at the Tower of London—if they ever leave, the whole place'll come crashing down. It's the same with Collier and Freekham!'

'Please,' said Sam, staring up at the heavens. '*Please!*'

'Collier taught my dad,' Ashley Lamb remarked. 'And my grandad.'

Ruth Cook glared across at Vicki Starling. 'And little Tweety Pie here sang like a canary to the Head and got him the boot.'

'I did not,' Vicki said coolly. 'He must have gone to the Head himself. Getting in first.'

'You mean getting *out* first,' said Sam.

Sara was glad that the rumours of Fido and Smithy's misdemeanour had already dwindled in importance. But she was less glad to find that as they entered their classroom, Janus was already waiting at her desk. She had the register open, her red pen poised like a dagger above the page.

'Sit down, all of you,' she snapped. She glared at Sam and Smithy as they sat down. Sara and Memphis had almost reached their seats in the corner when she spoke again. 'Except it's not all of you, is it? Where is Dorian Tennant?'

No one spoke.

'You, girl!' Janus stared at Sara, the big engagement ring on her left hand glowing in the sunlight like a third eye. 'What trouble is he up to now?'

'No trouble, miss.'

 148

She rose and walked slowly over. 'A likely tale.'

'He's with Mr Steen, miss,' said Sara nervously. 'Looking for the tape of our Social Studies lesson. You know, for that big meeting—'

'His . . . big . . . meeting . . .' For a moment, Janus looked as if she might explode. 'You're a supply teacher, easy come, easy go,' she said, mimicking Steen's voice, 'but *I'm* trying to build a career here . . .'

Sara frowned at her. 'Miss?'

'HA!' Janus suddenly thundered. 'Everyone thinks supply teachers have it easy! Well, we don't! The pressure we're under, the stick we get . . .' She looked around wildly, then seemed to realize she'd gone too far. Trying to compose herself, ignoring the looks of alarm and dismay, she returned to her desk and started taking the register as if nothing had happened.

'That woman is one eyeshadow short of a make-up set,' whispered Memphis.

'She's a supply teacher on the edge,' Sara agreed. 'I can't believe we've got her for Drama next!'

'Well, don't forget she's a professional actor, *dah-ling*,' Memphis grinned. 'Maybe she'll surprise us by playing the part of a sane teacher for five minutes.'

Sara stared at her. '*What* did you say?'

'I said she'd surprise us by—'

'You're a genius,' Sara told her.

'And you're not making much sense.'

'Nothing's made sense today,' said Sara, a slow smile spreading over her face as she looked over at Janus. 'Until now.'

Periods Seven and Eight
(Big) Drama

As he trudged along with the nervous class to the drama studio, Sam wondered what had happened to Fido. He was a no-show right the way through registration. And he wasn't waiting outside when they reached the studio either.

'What's taking him?' Sam turned to Smithy as the class lined up outside, waiting for Janus to let them in. 'It's not like he *really* had to find the tape.'

'He must be helping Steen dub down the role-playing stuff we did this morning on to video,' said Sara, 'in time for his big meeting.'

'I hope you're right,' said Smithy. 'Brucie was searching for the tape by the crash mats too, remember? He might have seen Fido with the tape and grabbed it!'

Memphis jabbed a finger at Janus, who shoved open the door and waved everyone through. 'If that was true, don't you reckon *she* would be in a better mood?'

Sam quite liked the drama studio, all black walls and backdrops and hanging drapes. The wooden floor was springy beneath your feet, and the acoustics were incredible—the tiniest noise really carried. Smithy had let go a massive fart once and it had echoed on for hours . . .

This lesson would *drag* on for hours, he decided. They were supposed to be doing some scenes from *Twelfth Night* by William Shakespeare, but Janus just perched on her chair staring into space, shifting uncomfortably in her tweedy suit as everyone sat down on the floor and got out their texts.

'Miss?' asked Sara, breaking the uneasy silence. 'Is it true that in Shakespeare's time, women weren't allowed to act on the stage?'

Janus stirred as if from a deep sleep. 'Yes, that's correct. It wasn't thought proper. All the women's parts were played by men.'

'Thought so,' said Sara.

Sam scoffed. 'Must have looked kind of weird.'

'Well, we've come a long way since then,' said Janus. Suddenly there was a knock at the door, and she jumped. 'Who is it?'

The door opened—and in walked Biggins the caretaker.

Sam swapped an incredulous look with Sara, wondering what would come next.

'Could I have a word, please, Mrs Janus?' He looked nervous, one of his pop-eyes twitching uncontrollably.

'What is it?'

'In private?'

A few 'Oooohs' and dirty titters went up from the class, as Janus followed Biggins outside into the corridor.

'No way am I missing this,' said Sam. He dashed over to the door, which was still open a crack, and pressed his ear to it. Sara and Smithy came up beside him to eavesdrop as well.

Janus was squaring up to Biggins. 'What is it?'

'Well, for a start I'd like my set of classroom keys back, please,' he said. 'When you sweet-talked me into letting you borrow them in period six, you said you'd give them back at the start of lunchtime.'

'So *that's* what she was up to with him,' Sara breathed. 'Persuading him to part with his keys!

 153

Me and Memphis saw them and we jumped to the wrong—'

'Shh,' Sam complained.

'. . . not supposed to lend them to anyone, see,' Biggins was saying. 'I could get in trouble.'

'Yes, well, sorry about that, but I was busy at lunchtime. Busier than I thought I'd be.' Janus handed him the keys back. 'Now, is that all?'

Clearly it wasn't. 'Did you find that scarf you were looking for?'

'Er—oh yes. Yes, I did.'

Sam shifted position and placed his eye to the crack in the door—in time to see Biggins produce a long tweed skirt and a flouncy top from behind his back.

'Only I wonder if this little lot went with it,' he said. 'These are yours, aren't they? I saw you wearing them yesterday.'

Janus was getting flustered. 'Um, yes. Yes, they are. But where did you find them?'

'In my hut, with some old PE equipment,' said Biggins gravely. 'But what would *you* be doing in there?'

'Oh . . . er . . . I must have left these clothes at

154

my brother's house,' she said quickly, snatching them back. 'And so . . . um . . . he brought them in for me . . . He's got keys to your hut, hasn't he? He must have left them in there by mistake.'

Sam turned to Smithy in consternation. 'I didn't expect to overhear a conversation like *this*!'

'They're like strangers!' Smithy scratched his head. 'Then, they—they can't be having an affair at all!'

'Which fits in with my theory completely,' said Sara, quite unruffled.

Behind them, their curious classmates were starting to chatter and snigger. Janus heard the noise and turned back to the door.

'Quick, get back!' Sam hissed, and all three jumped away and ran back to join the group. Janus steamed back inside just as their bums slapped the wooden floor. Showing off, Smithy had even managed to open his copy of *Twelfth Night* and now stared at it studiously.

Memphis leaned forwards. 'It would make more sense if you weren't reading it upside down.'

'Wouldn't be so sure about that,' Smithy murmured, flipping it round.

 155

Janus swiftly stowed the clothes under her chair as if nothing untoward had happened. But then there was another knock at the door.

'Who is it *this* time?' Janus growled.

Uh-oh, thought Sam. Her favourite people in the whole world came through the door—Mr Steen and Fido. And Fido was proudly wielding his camcorder.

'You two,' she said, her low voice lingering on the vowel sounds so the words seemed to last for a full minute.

'Afternoon, Mrs Janus,' said Steen, looking a little more relaxed than he had when they'd seen him last. 'Sorry Fido's late. I had to borrow him.'

Fido winked at Sam and Smithy.

'*Borrow* him, Mr Steen?' she said icily.

'Yeah, he's been helping me transfer the camcorder footage I took this morning on to a videotape.' Steen smiled. 'It was a close run thing, but now I've got something to show my visitors after all!'

'What!' Janus jumped in the air as if a small spike had just shot up her bottom. 'You found the camcorder tape?'

'Yeah, amazing bit of luck! Clever old Fido

156

found it by the litter bin beside the crash mats.'
Steen shrugged. 'Can't think how your brother
missed it—he'd already given up and gone in by
the time we arrived.'

'Knew it,' said Sara quietly, watching intently.

'So you found it,' said Janus uneasily. 'And
. . . you *watched* it?'

'Well, we fast-searched through a lot of it,'
Steen admitted. 'No changing rooms in sight, so
that's good news. Mainly Smithy mucking about,
nothing too incriminating.'

'Nothing *too* incriminating?' Her eyes
narrowed. 'You saw me, didn't you?'

'What, in the caretaker's hut, you mean?' said
Fido brightly. 'I suppose I might have pointed
that bit out . . .'

'Nice work, Fido!' Sam murmured, as a whispered wave of gossip and chatter swept through
the class. This was edge-of-the-seat stuff, even if
they *were* all sitting on the floor. Something juicy
was clearly afoot.

Steen blushed bright red. 'Like I told Fido, I
really don't think it's any of my business what
you—'

'You know, don't you! You know about me!'

'Mrs Janus, this is hardly the time and place to discuss such a matter.' Flustered, Steen glanced back out into the corridor. 'I just thought I'd quickly square things with you about Fido showing up late. Now, if you'll excuse me—'

'Don't play the innocent,' she said fiercely. 'I know you've tumbled me! Even after all I've done to cover it up!'

'Mrs Janus, really . . .' Again, Steen glanced out into the corridor, a little more anxiously now. 'I'm afraid I really have to go!'

'And that's the naked truth, miss,' added Fido with a cheeky gleam in his eye.

'Is everything all right, Mr Steen?' A concerned-looking man in a suit appeared in the doorway.

'Only we heard raised voices,' said a matronly woman, also smartly dressed, just behind him.

'Who are they?' cried Janus.

'These are my visitors,' said Steen, sending several apologetic smiles in their direction. 'Mr Young and Mrs Russell. They're psychoanalysts.'

Janus gasped. 'They're *what*!'

'Well, school therapists, really,' said Mrs Russell, smiling. 'And you are . . . ?'

'Perfectly all right, thank you very much!' Janus said shrilly. 'Keep away! I don't need a therapist!'

'No one said you did, Mrs Janus!' Steen protested.

Sam stared in disbelief. 'She's acting like a freak! What's wrong with her?'

'I so nearly got away with it!' Janus wailed. 'If it wasn't for those wretched boys and their wretched little tape . . . Well, you're not sending me to the Head's office. No way!' Suddenly she turned and bolted for the back of the drama studio in a blind panic. *So* blind, in fact, that she didn't seem to see that her pupils were in her path! Sam dived desperately aside, but it was too late.

Janus tripped over Sam's legs and went flying.

Her skirt flapped up in the air—to reveal a pair of men's underpants.

Her hair flew off and landed in Vicki Starling's lap. Vicki picked up the wig in horrified disbelief, then started to scream—setting off her three-strong clone club, Elise, Denise, and Therese, who all joined her in a caterwauling quartet.

'Ouch!' Janus yelled, landing flat on her face, her jacket and blouse rucked up around her—to reveal a striped rugby jersey beneath.

Everyone gathered round the fallen teacher in a shocked, bewildered silence.

Mr Young approached, crouching beside the prone figure like a doctor. Then he turned uncertainly to Steen. 'You did say . . . *Mrs* Janus?'

'Mrs? Not likely,' said Sara, as Young carefully rolled over the body. 'That's Mr Bruce!'

Sam gasped as he saw it was true. Suddenly, it seemed so obvious. Bruce and Janus had never been seen together—and here was the reason why. Where the piled-high hair had once been, a familiar sandy crewcut was now visible. The rugby jersey was the one worn by Bruce just this lunchtime—he must have put the blouse on over it to save time changing. And the pants were bloke's pants because, however confused Brucie was, at the end of the day he *was* a bloke.

'I don't need a therapist!' he insisted.

'But he *seriously* needs a stylist,' Memphis declared, 'and fast!'

'Mr Bruce . . .' Like everyone else, Steen was staring at the dishevelled figure in disbelief. 'What's going on?'

'I'm not crazy!' Bruce said, propping himself up on his elbows. 'I'm just . . .' He sighed. 'I'm just a frustrated actor. I'm only doing supply teaching to pay the bills—till I get my big break in the theatre!'

'Does breaking a leg in a drama studio count?' Sam wondered.

'Go on, Mr Bruce,' said Mrs Russell soothingly. 'Let it all out.'

'I'm not just *one* supply teacher, you see. I play lots of different teachers at different schools!' He gave a mad giggle. 'It keeps me busy, and it means I still get to act! For instance, there's a German teacher I do—Herr Wagner, his name is. I play him with an eyepatch and a beard! You should see him!'

Smithy turned up his nose. 'No, ta.'

'But why take the risk of playing two teachers here at once?' asked Steen.

Brucie's eye had started to twitch. 'It was to be my most demanding performance,' he whispered. 'You see, Freekham was *desperate* for teachers after that food poisoning incident, and I could not resist the challenge—or the double salary! But it's been such hard work. Teaching drama . . . running about on the playing fields . . . trying to keep my secret safe . . . Well, it's enough to make me . . .'

Suddenly Brucie flopped backwards in a faint.

'Fascinating!' Russell turned to Young. 'I'd say it's a good job we discovered this ruse when we did. If this man had kept on playing all these different parts . . .'

Young nodded. 'The strain could have proved too much. He might even have suffered a nervous breakdown!'

'She—he—has certainly been acting strangely today,' said Steen.

Then Brucie groaned and looked around him in a daze. 'What happened? Where am I? *Who* am I?'

Steen held a hand out to Brucie, who took it dazedly. 'Come on, mate,' he said. 'We'll go and see the headmaster, then we'll arrange for you to have a little time off.'

'Oh, yes, I could use a holiday,' Brucie agreed. 'And so could Belinda . . .'

'I'm so sorry about this,' Steen told his VIP guests. 'I know you're ever so busy, and we haven't even started our meeting—'

'Oh, we'll make time for that, don't you worry,' said Young with a delighted smile. 'This has been absolutely fascinating! Mind if we tag along with you to the Head? Perhaps we can all discuss your proposals for this SHAPE club together!'

Steen beamed with pleasure. 'Be my guest!'

'And mine!' squawked Mr Bruce in his Janus voice. '*Und* mine!' he added in a thick German accent.

'I'll arrange for another teacher to come here and supervise you lot,' Steen told the class. 'In the meantime, behave yourselves—and keep the noise down.'

No one spoke, or even seemed to breathe, until Steen's little group had departed and the door clicked quietly shut behind them.

Then pandemonium broke out. Thirty conversations started at once.

'What was *that* about—!'

'Brucie's a gender-bender!'

'He's mental!'

'What shall we do with his wig?'

But while the scandalized chatter went on, Sam, Smithy, Fido, and Memphis all gathered around Sara expectantly.

'You *knew* that Brucie and Janus were the same person, didn't you?' said Sam accusingly.

163

'I only really worked it out in afternoon registration,' she admitted. 'That's when he gave himself away.'

'How?' said Memphis.

'"Janus" quoted something that Steen had said, word for word,' she revealed. 'But it was something he told *Mr Bruce*—I heard them outside the changing rooms! So how would "she" have known?'

'Brucie might have told her,' Fido pointed out.

'Ah,' Sara smiled, clearly enjoying this, 'but then there's all the *other* evidence . . .'

'How about we backtrack a bit,' said Smithy. 'Let me get this straight. "Janus" had her kit off in the caretaker's hut when we caught her on tape—*not* because she was having a fling with Biggins, but because she was changing to look like Mr Bruce again, right?'

'Right,' said Sara. 'I guess it was the perfect place to use for quick changes when Biggins was out the way. It was off the beaten track, private —and since Brucie was the Games teacher, he had his own key!'

'If only we'd been taping a few moments later,' groaned Fido. 'We'd have got him taking his wig off and known everything straight away. I felt sure she must be having a fling with Biggins!'

'The facts seemed to fit,' Sara agreed, 'until I looked at them closely.'

'Sherlock Knot,' said Sam drily.

She shrugged. 'Thing was, Brucie didn't know for sure if you had any more evidence on tape—maybe something that would really incriminate him. That's why he *had* to get the tape back, whatever it took.'

'But at the end of the day, he wasn't man enough for the task,' declared Fido.

'You mean he wasn't *woman* enough,' smiled Memphis. 'Hang on, though. When we saw Bruce go into the caretaker's hut during Games, he was changing into Janus, right?'

'Right,' said Sam, 'because it was Janus who almost caught us in the classroom.'

'And Janus who we saw borrowing the keys off Biggins,' Sara agreed.

'But why go to all that trouble?' asked Memphis. 'Why not sneak off as Brucie?'

Sam reckoned he knew. 'Because if a teacher had seen him, Brucie might have got done for bunking off. They'd have known he wasn't supervising us lot in Games. But since Janus must have had a free period or whatever, she could go where she wanted.'

'Makes sense,' Memphis conceded.

'But Brucie nearly slipped up when he got changed back in time to welcome us back from our run,' said Sara. 'Remember how he was holding his left hand and reckoned he'd sprained it?'

'And then later on it was fine again, uh-huh,' sighed Smithy. 'You're obsessed about that hand!'

'He wasn't holding it 'cause he'd hurt it at all,' Sara told them triumphantly. 'He was holding it to cover up the fact he'd *forgotten to take off Janus's rings* in his rush to get changed back again!'

'Of course.' Memphis groaned; closed her eyes. 'It's obvious once you realize.'

Sam nodded. 'Like the way he faked that call on his mobile from "his sister" about Fido and Smithy taping the girls' changing rooms—he was giving himself an excuse to confiscate the tape and the camcorder right away.'

'And I bet he let Cassie Shaw overhear on purpose,' Fido realized. 'So she'd spread it about and make the story sound more convincing!'

'Cassie still believes it now,' said Smithy worriedly.

Sara smiled reassuringly. 'I'm sure when the Head knows the score he'll put people straight.'

'Speaking of putting people straight,' said Fido, pulling the camcorder tape from his pocket. 'I guess we should let Biggins know we've wiped his little outburst in the hut.'

'Just think,' said Smithy. 'If we hadn't been filming those stunts, Brucie-Janus would have kept his little secret!'

'Like that woman said, probably best for his head in the long run,' Sam reflected.

Memphis was grinning, her catlike eyes agleam. 'Well, hey, boys, you can tell Biggins what you've wiped right now,' she said. 'Look who's come to babysit . . .'

Sam turned to find the door to the drama studio had swung open. 'The *caretaker's* taking us for Drama?'

'Afraid you'll have to put up with me taking you,' said Biggins, a bit self-consciously. 'There aren't any teachers going spare and . . . Well, well.' He gave a horrid smile at the sight of Fido and Smithy. 'It's you two again.'

Sara nudged Fido.

'Yes, sir—but . . . er . . . you don't have to worry about us any longer.' He started fast-forwarding through the tape. 'We thought it was only fair to wipe the tape of you—er . . . *talking* to us. Hang on . . . yes! Here, look.'

He passed the camcorder to Biggins. Its little screen showed Smithy in the hut—then nothing but white fuzz.

Biggins smiled grimly. 'Much obliged, boys.'

'That's all sorted, then,' said Smithy.

'Er . . . can I have my camcorder back, please, sir?' asked Fido.

'No,' beamed Biggins. He hit the rewind and then turned to the rest of the class.

'Right, open your books, please, all of you. You're in luck. I've seen *Twelfth Night*, you know. Freekham Town Hall Players, 1986. My wife played Second Attendant. We'll look at Act One. Scene Five, just after Malvolio exits . . .' He jabbed a thick finger at Fido. 'You can play Olivia, and you—' he jabbed another finger at Smithy—'can play Viola.'

'I'd sooner play truant!' Fido spluttered. 'Sir, those are . . . *girls*' parts!'

'And we don't have girls' parts!' added Smithy.

'Thought a pair of scallies like you would be up for anything!' retorted Biggins. 'Now, get up in front of the class and get reading—*ladies*!'

Ruth had seized hold of Brucie's skirt and blouse from under the teacher's chair. 'They can wear these!' she sniggered. 'They're big enough for two, and I don't reckon Janus will need them for a while!'

'Better than that, there are some proper dresses in the props box!' said Vicki Starling helpfully. 'Shall I get them?'

'That's a great idea!' beamed Biggins. 'Get 'em on, boys!'

Smithy and Fido started trembling as Vicki and Ruthless approached waving hideous pink silk dresses in their faces. The rest of the class were cracking up, and none louder than Sara and Memphis.

'This is a nightmare,' Fido groaned, as he struggled into the smock.

'It's not fair!' Smithy cried, trying to work out if he should step into the dress or pull it on over his head.

 169

'Oh, come on, guys,' laughed Sam. 'With Brucie and Janus on your backs all day, you must have picked up *some* tips!'

'Yeah,' said Fido with feeling. 'Here's one— never bring your camcorder into school.'

'Good,' said Biggins, flicking the camcorder into record mode. 'But since it's here, let's film this little performance for posterity!'

Fido and Smithy swapped looks of pure horror as a gale of laughter raged around them.

'Noooooooooo . . . !'

HOMETIME

'Fido wasn't a bad Olivia, was he?' said Sam.

'He's a better Fido,' Sara decided.

Memphis nodded with feeling. 'And he looked even worse than Smithy in that dress.'

They were loitering at the top of the school drive, waiting for Fido and Smithy to show. Sam glanced over at the caretaker's hut and smiled to himself. Biggins's crazy casting had given them the funniest Drama lesson of all time—but at the end of it, the guys had been summoned to the Head's office. Sam and Sara wanted to be sure everything was OK, and Memphis was happy to hang around.

'Hey, look,' said Sam. 'It's Linus Smellick and . . . what was his name?'

'Oscar Donahue!' called Oscar crossly.

The two younger boys were picking up litter from the grass verges, stuffing it into a big bin liner.

Memphis smiled. 'Glad Collier's got them doing something useful on their after-school detention.'

'Speak of the devil . . .' said Sara.

Sam followed her gaze to see Killer Collier shuffling along towards Linus and Oscar. 'You boys,' he said. 'I told you to report to my class-room after school for a detention.'

Linus stared at him, lip trembling. 'But—but we *did*, sir!'

Oscar raised the rubbish sack. 'You told us to come out here and collect litter, sir!'

'Nonsense, boy! The two of you are skiving off, it's obvious!'

'But—'

'No buts!' Collier boomed. 'You'll finish up here, then come to see me again tomorrow so I can set you *another* punishment. And don't think I'll forget about *that*!' Leaving Linus and Oscar to stare miserably after him, Collier headed back off towards the school. Sam spotted something suspiciously like a small spring in his step. 'Oh, yes indeed,' the old boy chuckled to himself. 'If I *have* to go, I'm going to damn well enjoy myself while I can!'

'Sneaky old goat,' Sam muttered, smiling.

'Hey, and here's not-so-Softy Steen!' said Sara, pointing to the multi-coloured figure walking over to his battered Volvo in the car park. 'Hey, sir!' she called. 'What happened with Mr Bruce? Is everything OK?'

'Everything's cool,' said Steen, changing his course to join them. 'Bruce admitted everything to the Head—including that made-up nonsense about the changing rooms.'

'So the Head's not hauled Fido and Smithy in to give them a—' Sam bit his tongue— 'a telling off, then, sir?'

'No, only to say that he'll clear up the rumours in a full school assembly tomorrow,' said Steen. 'The telling off will come from *me* for getting into that fight at lunchtime—and you'll get it too, I'm afraid.'

'Yeah, we reckoned we would,' said Sara.

'Is Mr Bruce going to prison?' Sam asked eagerly.

Steen frowned and shook his head. 'He's going to take a very, very long holiday. Then he plans to sell his story to the press, and use the publicity to relaunch his acting career!'

173

'No one would ever believe a story like that!' Sam scoffed. 'They wouldn't give him fifty p for it!'

'Well, in any case, my visiting VIPs reckon he'll make a full recovery.'

'Oh yeah,' said Sara, remembering. 'How did your meeting go in the end?'

'It was all cool—thanks to Mr Bruce,' smiled Steen. 'Stumbling upon such an interesting looper put them in a really good mood. They enjoyed the tape of your workshops and loved the idea of SHAPE. The club's going county-wide as of the autumn term!'

Memphis raised her eyebrows. 'That's, uh, nice.'

'Yeah. Like, totally great,' said Sara.

'If you weren't giving us detentions, we'd be a lot happier for you, sir,' Sam explained.

'Thanks, mate!' grinned Steen. 'Well, got to run, guys. Try to stay out of trouble from now on, 'K?'

Sam, Sara, and Memphis all looked at each other. ''K,' they told him in unison.

'Well, that's Steen's career looking a lot rosier,' Sara observed.

'Better for him if it had all gone horribly wrong,' sighed Sam. 'He could have left teaching and gone on to better things. You know, retrained as a sewage attendant, or a toilet cleaner or something. Now the poor sap's stuck in schools for life . . .'

'Speaking of poor saps,' said Memphis. 'The waiting's over. Here they come!'

Fido and Smithy were swaggering along the path towards them, Fido, as ever, with his camcorder at the ready.

'Hey, Fido, it's our adoring fans,' said Smithy.

Fido looked at Sam and turned up his nose. 'Don't fancy yours much.'

'Ha, ha,' said Sam. 'You're not wearing that dress now you know.'

'Steen told us the Head's going to clean up your reputations tomorrow,' said Sara. 'Was he cool about it all?'

'Yeah, it was OK!' Smithy admitted, fetching his racer from the bike sheds nearby.

'Once he found out what Brucie had been saying, he was very understanding,' Fido explained.

'It's just a shame Biggins wasn't! He rewound

175

the tape in the camcorder back to the beginning, and recorded our cross-dressing Shakespeare over the top!'

Memphis smiled. 'Over the top is right!'

'Ouch!' said Sam, wincing. 'So after all we went through to keep hold of that tape—we've lost all your stunt footage anyway!'

Sara smiled. 'But at least we've still got a record of Fido and Smithy glammed up for *Twelfth Night* as you've never seen it before!'

'I'm not letting Casey show *that* on the *Camcorder Catastrophes* show,' Smithy declared, wheeling his bike over. 'It's so not fair. I could almost feel that two hundred quid fee burning a hole in my pocket . . .'

'Leave it to smoulder,' Fido advised, a sneaky smile on his face. 'Because we didn't come out of this *total* losers.'

'We didn't?'

'Nope.'

Everyone stared at Fido, waiting for the punchline.

Sam slapped his arm. 'Well, come on then!'

'Oh, it's no big deal.' Fido was milking the moment for all it was worth. 'But Biggins didn't tape over *absolutely* everything. One little gem is left—right at the end of the tape. When we came into the Drama studio and Brucie went crazy, I thought I should set the camcorder going . . .'

Sam grinned. 'You mean—?'

'I recorded Brucie doing his spectacular stunt fall,' laughed Fido, patting his camcorder proudly. 'Wig flying off, pants on display . . . the works!'

'YES!' Smithy punched the air. 'Casey's bound to show a clip like that—it's pure gold!'

Fido whooped. 'Pure two hundred quid, you mean!'

'Glad to hear it, boys,' called a rough voice from behind them.

Sam and the others stopped laughing, and turned to face Connor Flint. He had come up behind them, flanked by his menacing mates.

'I've got detention all next week,' he said, 'and all for something I never done.'

'Uh, sorry about that,' said Smithy.

'So I reckon maybe I deserve some compensation.' Connor smiled, showing those scary sharp teeth. 'Say, three-quarters of the cash you'll get if that TV show shows this oh-so-funny clip of yours.'

'Three-quarters?' squeaked Fido.

Connor clenched his fists. 'Or else you *could* pay us back with punchbag practice.'

Smithy laughed weakly. 'Three-quarters sounds very fair. More than fair!'

Memphis was quick to prick their bubble. 'It'll never be shown anyway, guys. You taped it without permission—if it went on TV, Brucie would probably sue you for damaging his character. Probably take the whole school to court or something!'

Fido frowned. 'He would?'

'Oh,' said Smithy. Then he looked at Fido and sighed. 'Well, at least we're only losing fifty quid now instead of two hundred!'

Connor's face had darkened. 'Well, you'd better not be thinking of sending in that clip of me bursting my trousers instead . . .'

'We couldn't even if we wanted to,' Fido informed him.

'Which we don't,' Smithy added quickly.

'No,' Fido agreed. 'It's been taped over, see.'

'Oh yeah?' Connor scowled. 'You expect me

178

to believe that? Give me the tape!'

'It's been taped over, honest! It's full of awful shots of me and Smithy wearing dresses and spouting Shakespeare's old rubbish!'

'Really? Well, maybe we'll get *that* on TV instead!' Connor advanced with his thuggish friends, holding out one hand, raising the other in a fist. 'Hand it over!'

'Not likely!' said Fido. He ran in one direction, and Smithy cycled off in the other. Once they'd cleared Connor's blockade, Fido jumped on the back of the bike and Smithy started pedalling for all he was worth.

'Get them!' Connor yelled, and the gang of lads hurtled off down the drive in hot pursuit.

Sam watched the frantic figures dwindle from view. 'Is that really the toughest lad in the school and his gang, chasing after a tape of two boys in dresses?'

'I think maybe it is,' said Memphis faintly. 'Then again, I think maybe I dreamed this whole day.'

'It was one weird day, all right,' said Sara.

Sam grinned. 'One to add to the collection . . . here at Freekham High.'

Steve Cole spent a happy childhood being loud and aspiring to amuse. At school his teachers often despaired of him—one of them went so far as to ban him from her English lessons, which enhanced his reputation no end.

Having grown up liking stories, he went to university to read more of them. A few years later he started writing them too. Steve has also worked as a researcher for radio and an editor of books and magazines for both children and adults. *One Weird Day at Freekham High: Ouch!* is his third novel for Oxford University Press.

JUST HOW WEIRD CAN ONE DAY BE?
YOU'RE ABOUT TO FIND OUT . . .

One Weird Day at FREEKHAM HIGH

THUMB
Steve Cole

It's the first day at a new school for both Sam and Sara.
So of course they're hoping to fit in quickly. All they want is a
helping **HAND**. Some new friends to keep an **EYE** out for
them and help them get a**HEAD**.

What they're probably *not* hoping for is a

THUMB.

Actually, a *lot* of thumbs. And fingers. They're turning up all
over Freekham High—in seriously unexpected places. But WHY?

Can Sam solve the mystery of the bothersome body parts?
Can Sara keep her cool in the face of the dastardly digits?
And most important, can they get through the day
without being labelled as losers by their new classmates?

ISBN: 0-19-275424-6

One Weird Day at FREEKHAM HIGH

Sock

Steve Cole

Something strange is going on at Freekham High.
Ginger Mutton was always the quiet, unpopular one.
Now everybody wants to hear what she has to say—
because she's started to predict the future. With a

Sock.

And **Sock**ingly enough, her predictions are coming true—
just not always to the right people! It **Seams** to be another
Darned Freekham mystery.

Can Sam and Sara get **Toe** the bottom of it before
people start getting hurt?

ISBN: 0-19-275425-4

One Weird Day at FREEKHAM HIGH

Pigeon

Steve Cole

Sara, Sam and friends are putting on a play—what could be more
harmless than that? It's going to be a nice, restful, fun day to
round off the summer term. But this is Freekham High, where
the unexpected always happens . . . And this time, it's a plague of

PIGEONS!

It's almost as if the birds have a grudge against the school,
dive-bombing windows and making a mess everywhere—it's
a **SOAR** point with some of the teachers. Meanwhile, Sara's
getting in a **FLAP** over a ghost in the storeroom and Fido's
FLYING off the handle when the actors' costumes go missing.
As strange setbacks **FLOCK** around them, will the
play **TAKE** OFF—or end in disaster and droppings?

ISBN: 0-19-275427-0